THE TOR DOUBLES

Tor is proud to bring you the best in science fiction's short novels. An amazing amount of particularly fine science fiction is written at a length just too short to put in a book by itself, so we're providing them two at a time.

The Tor Doubles will be both new stories and older ones, all carefully chosen. Whichever side you start with, you will be able to turn the book over and enjoy the other side just as much.

TANGO CHARLIE COULD NOT BE BOARDED.

It could be destroyed. But things could leave *Tango Charlie. It would only be necessary to withdraw the robot probes that had watched so long and faithfully, and the survivors could be evacuated.*

That left the main question. Should they *be evacuated?*

(The fact that only one survivor had been sighted so far was not mentioned. Everyone assumed others would show up sooner or later. After all, it was simply not possible that just one eight-year-old girl could be the only occupant of a station no one had entered or left for thirty years.)

Wilhelm, obviously upset but clinging strongly to her position, advocated blowing up the station at once. There was some support for this, but only about ten percent of the group.

The eventual decision was to do nothing at the moment.

After all, there were almost five whole days to keep thinking about it.

THE TOR DOUBLE NOVELS

*forthcoming

JOHN VARLEY

TANGO CHARLIE AND FOXTROT ROMEO

TOR®

A TOM DOHERTY ASSOCIATES BOOK
NEW YORK

TANGO CHARLIE AND FOXTROT ROMEO

Copyright © 1986 by John Varley

Reprinted by permission of the author and his agents, Kirby McCauley, Ltd.

A TOR Book
Published by Tom Doherty Associates, Inc.
49 West 24 Street
New York, N.Y. 10010

Cover art by David Lee Anderson

ISBN: 0-812-55956-8   Can. ISN: 0-812-55957-6

First Tor edition: January 1989

Printed in the United States of America

0 9 8 7 6 5 4 3 2 1

The police probe was ten kilometers from Tango Charlie's Wheel when it made rendezvous with the unusual corpse. At this distance, the wheel was still an imposing presence, blinding white against the dark sky, turning in perpetual sunlight. The probe was often struck by its beauty, by the myriad ways the wheel caught the light in its thousand and one windows. It had been composing a thought-poem around that theme when the corpse first came to its attention.

There was a pretty irony about the probe. Less than a meter in diameter, it was equipped with sensitive radar, very good visible-light camera eyes, and a dim awareness. Its sentient qualities came from a walnut-sized lump of human brain tissue cultured in a lab. This was the cheapest and simplest way to endow a machine with certain human qualities that were often useful in spying devices. The part of the brain used was the part humans use to appreciate beautiful

1

things. While the probe watched, it dreamed endless beautiful dreams. No one knew this but the probe's control, which was a computer that had not bothered to tell anyone about it. The computer did think it was rather sweet, though.

There were many instructions the probe had to follow. It did so religiously. It was never to approach the wheel more closely than five kilometers. All objects larger than one centimeter leaving the wheel were to be pursued, caught, and examined. Certain categories were to be reported to higher authorities. All others were to be vaporized by the probe's small battery of lasers. In thirty years of observation, only a dozen objects had needed reporting. All of them proved to be large structural components of the wheel which had broken away under the stress of rotation. Each had been destroyed by the probe's larger brother, on station five hundred kilometers away.

When it reached the corpse, it immediately identified it that far: it was a dead body, frozen in a vaguely fetal position. From there on, the probe got stuck.

Many details about the body did not fit the acceptable parameters for such a thing. The probe examined it again, and still again, and kept coming up with the same unacceptable answers. It could not tell what the body was ... and yet it was a body.

The probe was so fascinated that its attention wavered for some time, and it was not as alert as it had been these previous years. So it was unprepared when the second falling object bumped gently against its metal hide. Quickly the probe leveled a camera eye at the second object. It was a single, long-stemmed, red rose, of a type that had once flourished in the wheel's florist shop.

Like the corpse, it was frozen solid. The impact had shattered some of the outside petals, which rotated slowly in a halo around the rose itself.

It was quite pretty. The probe resolved to compose a thought-poem about it when this was all over. The probe photographed it, vaporized it with its lasers—all according to instruction—then sent the picture out on the airwaves along with a picture of the corpse, and a frustrated shout.

"Help!" the probe cried, and sat back to await developments.

"A puppy?" Captain Hoeffer asked, arching one eyebrow dubiously.

"A Shetland Sheepdog puppy, sir," said Corporal Anna-Louise Bach, handing him the batch of holos of the enigmatic orbiting object, and the single shot of the shattered rose. He took them, leafed through them rapidly, puffing on his pipe.

"And it came from Tango Charlie?"

"There is no possible doubt about it, sir."

Bach stood at parade rest across the desk from her seated superior and cultivated a detached gaze. I'm only awaiting orders, she told herself. I have no opinions of my own. I'm brimming with information, as any good recruit should be, but I will offer it only when asked, and then I will pour it forth until asked to stop.

That was the theory, anyway. Bach was not good at it. It was her ineptitude at humoring incompetence in superiors that had landed her in this assignment, and put her in contention for the title of oldest living recruit/apprentice in the New Dresden Police Department.

"A Shetland ..."

"Sheepdog, sir." She glanced down at him, and interpreted the motion of his pipestem to mean he wanted to know more. "A variant of the Collie, developed on the Shetland Isles of Scotland. A working dog, very bright, gentle, good with children."

"You're an authority on dogs, Corporal Bach?"

"No, sir. I've only seen them in the zoo. I took the liberty of researching this matter before bringing it to your attention, sir."

He nodded, which she hoped was a good sign. "What else did you learn?"

"They come in three varieties: black, blue merle, and sable. They were developed from Icelandic and Greenland stock, with infusions of Collie and possible Spaniel genes. Specimens were first shown at Cruft's in London in 1906, and in American—"

"No, no. I don't give a damn about Shelties."

"Ah. We have confirmed that there were four Shelties present on Tango Charlie at the time of the disaster. They were being shipped to the zoo at Clavius. There were no other dogs of any breed resident at the station. We haven't determined how it is that their survival was overlooked during the investigation of the tragedy."

"Somebody obviously missed them."

"Yes, sir."

Hoeffer jabbed at a holo with his pipe.

"What's this? Have you researched *that* yet?"

Bach ignored what she thought might be sarcasm. Hoeffer was pointing to the opening in the animal's side.

"The computer believes it to be a birth defect sir. The skin is not fully formed. It left an opening into the gut."

"And what's this?"

"Intestines. The bitch would lick the puppy clean after birth. When she found this malformation, she would keep licking as long as she tasted blood. The intestines were pulled out, and the puppy died."

"It couldn't have lived anyway. Not with that hole."

"No, sir. If you'll notice, the forepaws are also malformed. The computer feels the puppy was stillborn."

Hoeffer studied the various holos in a blue cloud of pipe smoke, then sighed and leaned back in his chair.

"It's fascinating, Bach. After all these years, there are dogs alive on Tango Charlie. And breeding, too. Thank you for bringing it to my attention."

Now it was Bach's turn to sigh. She *hated* this part. Now it was her job to explain it to him.

"It's even more fascinating than that, sir. We knew Tango Charlie was largely pressurized. So it's understandable that a colony of dogs could breed there. But, barring an explosion, which would have spread a large amount of debris into the surrounding space, this dead puppy must have left the station through an airlock."

His face clouded, and he looked at her in gathering outrage.

"Are you saying ... there are humans alive aboard Tango Charlie?"

"Sir, it has to be that ... or some *very* intelligent dogs."

Dogs can't count.

Charlie kept telling herself that as she knelt on the edge of forever and watched little Albert dwindling, hurrying out to join the whirling stars. She wondered if he would become a star himself. It seemed possible.

She dropped the rose after him and watched it dwindle, too. Maybe it would become a rosy star.

She cleared her throat. She had thought of things to say, but none of them sounded good. So she decided on a hymn, the only one she knew, taught her long ago by her mother, who used to sing it for her father, who was a spaceship pilot. Her voice was clear and true.

> *"Lord guard and guide all those who fly*
> *Through Thy great void above the sky.*
> *Be with them all on ev'ry flight,*
> *In radiant day or darkest night.*
> *Oh, hear our prayer, extend Thy grace*
> *To those in peril deep in space."*

She knelt silently for a while, wondering if God was listening, and if the hymn was good for dogs, too. Albert sure was flying through the void, so it seemed to Charlie he ought to be deserving of some grace.

Charlie was perched on a sheet of twisted metal on the bottom, or outermost layer of the wheel. There was no gravity anywhere in the wheel, but since it was spinning, the farther down you went the heavier you felt. Just beyond the sheet of metal was a void, a hole ripped in the wheel's outer skin, fully twenty meters across. The metal had been twisted out and down by the force of some long-ago explosion, and this part of the wheel was a good place to walk carefully, if you had to walk here at all.

She picked her way back to the airlock, let herself in, and sealed the outer door behind her. She knew it was useless, knew there was nothing but vacuum on the other side, but it was something that had been impressed on her very strongly. When you go through a door, you lock it behind you. Lock it tight. If you don't, the breathsucker will get you in the middle of the night.

She shivered, and went to the next lock, which also led only to vacuum, as did the one beyond that. Finally, at the fifth airlock, she stepped into a tiny room that had breathable atmosphere, if a little chilly. Then she went through yet another lock before daring to take off her helmet.

At her feet was a large plastic box, and inside it, resting shakily on a scrap of bloody blanket and not at all at peace with the world, were two puppies. She picked them up, one in each hand—which didn't make them any happier—and nodded in satisfaction.

She kissed them, and put them back in the box. Tucking it under her arm, she faced another door. She could hear claws scratching at this one.

"Down, Fuchsia," she shouted. "Down, mommadog." The scratching stopped, and she opened the last door and stepped through.

Fuchsia O'Charlie Station was sitting obediently, her ears pricked up, her head cocked and her eyes alert with that total, quivering concentration only a mother dog can achieve.

"I've got 'em, Foosh," Charlie said. She went down on one knee and allowed Fuchsia to put her paws up on the edge of the box. "See? There's Helga, and there's Conrad, and there's Albert, and there's Conrad, and Helga. One, two, three, four, eleventy-nine and six makes twenty-seven. See?"

Fuchsia looked at them doubtfully, then leaned in to pick one up, but Charlie pushed her away.

"I'll carry them," she said, and they set out along the darkened corridor. Fuchsia kept her eyes on the box, whimpering with the desire to get to her pups.

Charlie called this part of the wheel The Swamp. Things had gone wrong here a long time ago, and the more time went by, the worse it got. She

figured it had been started by the explosion—
which, in its turn, had been an indirect result of
The Dying. The explosion had broken important
pipes and wires. Water had started to pool in the
corridor. Drainage pumps kept it from turning
into an impossible situation. Charlie didn't come
here very often.

Recently plants had started to grow in the
swamp. They were ugly things, corpse-white or
dental-plaque-yellow or mushroom gray. There
was very little light for them, but they didn't
seem to mind. She sometimes wondered if they
were plants at all. Once she thought she had seen
a fish. It had been white and blind. Maybe it had
been a toad. She didn't like to think of that.

Charlie sloshed through the water, the box of
puppies under one arm and her helmet under the
other. Fuchsia bounced unhappily along with her.

At last they were out of it, and back into
regions she knew better. She turned right and
went three flights up a staircase—dogging the
door behind her at every landing—then out into
the Promenade Deck, which she called home.

About half the lights were out. The carpet was
wrinkled and musty, and worn in the places
Charlie frequently walked. Parts of the walls were
streaked with water stains, or grew mildew in
leprous patches. Charlie seldom noticed these
things unless she was looking through her pictures from the old days, or was coming up from
the maintenance levels, as she was now. Long
ago, she had tried to keep things clean, but the
place was just too big for a little girl. Now she
limited her housekeeping to her own living
quarters—and like any little girl, sometimes forgot about that, too.

She stripped off her suit and stowed it in the
locker where she always kept it, then padded a

short way down the gentle curve of the corridor to the Presidential Suite, which was hers. As she entered, with Fuchsia on her heels, a long-dormant television camera mounted high on the wall stuttered to life. Its flickering red eye came on, and it turned jerkily on its mount.

Anna-Louise Bach entered the darkened monitoring room, mounted the five stairs to her office at the back, sat down, and put her bare feet up on her desk. She tossed her uniform cap, caught it on one foot, and twirled it idly there. She laced her fingers together, leaned her chin on them, and thought about it.

Corporal Steiner, her number two on C Watch, came up to the platform, pulled a chair close, and sat beside her.

"Well? How did it go?"

"You want some coffee?" Bach asked him. When he nodded, she pressed a button in the arm of her chair. "Bring two coffees to the Watch Commander's station. Wait a minute . . . bring a pot, and two mugs." She put her feet down and turned to face him.

"He did figure out there had to be a human aboard."

Steiner frowned. "You must have given him a clue."

"Well, I mentioned the airlock angle."

"See? He'd never have seen it without that."

"All right. Call it a draw."

"So then what did our leader want to do?"

Bach had to laugh. Hoeffer was unable to find his left testicle without a copy of *Gray's Anatomy*.

"He came to a quick decision. We had to send a ship out there *at once*, find the survivors and bring them to New Dresden with all possible speed."

"And then you reminded him ..."

"... that no ship had been allowed to get within five kilometers of Tango Charlie for thirty years. That even our probe had to be small, slow, and careful to operate in the vicinity, and that if it crossed the line it would be destroyed, too. He was all set to call the Oberluftwaffe and ask for a cruiser. I pointed out that A, we already *had* a robot cruiser on station under the reciprocal trade agreement with *Allgemein Fernsehen Gesellschaft;* B, that it was perfectly capable of defeating Tango Charlie without any more help; but C, any battle like that would *kill* whoever was on Charlie; but that in any case, D, even if a ship *could* get to Charlie there was a good reason for not doing so."

Emil Steiner winced, pretending pain ·in the head.

"Anna, Anna, you should never list things to him like that, and if you do, you should *never* get to point D."

"Why not?"

"Because you're lecturing him. If you have to make a speech like that, make it a set of options, which I'm sure you've already seen, sir, but which I will list for you, sir, to get all our ducks in a row. Sir."

Bach grimaced, knowing he was right. She was too impatient.

The coffee arrived, and while they poured and took the first sips, she looked around the big monitoring room. This is where impatience gets you.

In some ways, it could have been a lot worse. It *looked* like a good job. Though only a somewhat senior Recruit/Apprentice Bach was in command of thirty other R/A's on her watch, and had the rank of Corporal. The working conditions were good: clean, high-tech surroundings, low job stress, the opportunity to command, however fleetingly. Even the coffee was good.

But it was a dead-end, and everyone knew it. It was a job many rookies held for a year or two before being moved on to more important and prestigious assignments: part of a routine career. When an R/A stayed in the monitoring room for five years, even as a watch commander, someone was sending her a message. Bach understood the message, had realized the problem long ago. But she couldn't seem to do anything about it. Her personality was too abrasive for routine promotions. Sooner or later she angered her commanding officers in one way or another. She was far too good for anything overtly negative to appear in her yearly evaluations. But there were ways such reports could be written, good things left un-said, a lack of excitement on the part of the reporting officer ... all things that added up to stagnation.

So here she was in Navigational Tracking, not really a police function at all, but something the New Dresden Police Department had handled for a hundred years and would probably handle for a hundred more.

It was a necessary job. So is garbage collection. But it was not what she had signed up for, ten years ago.

Ten years! God, it sounded like a long time. Any of the skilled guilds were hard to get into, but the average apprenticeship in New Dresden was six years.

She put down her coffee cup and picked up a hand mike.

"Tango Charlie, this is Foxtrot Romeo. Do you read?"

She listened, and heard only background hiss.

Her troops were trying every available channel with the same message, but this one had been the main channel back when TC-38 had been a going concern.

"Tango Charlie, this is Foxtrot Romeo. Come in, please."

Again, nothing.

Steiner put his cup close to hers, and leaned back in his chair.

"So did he remember what the reason was? Why we can't approach?"

"He did, eventually. His first step was to slap a top-priority security rating on the whole affair, and he was confident the government would back him up."

"We got that part. The alert came through about twenty minutes ago."

"I figured it wouldn't do any harm to let him send it. He needed to do something. And it's what I would have done."

"It's what you *did*, as soon as the pictures came in."

"You know I don't have the authority for that."

"Anna, when you get that look in your eye and say, 'If one of you bastards breathes a word of this to *anyone*, I will cut out your tongue and eat it for breakfast,' . . . well, people listen."

"Did I say that?"

"Your very words."

"No wonder they all love me so much."

She brooded on that for a while, until T/A3 Klosinski hurried up the steps to her office.

"Corporal Bach, we've finally seen something," he said.

Bach looked at the big semicircle of flat television screens, over three hundred of them, on the wall facing her desk. Below the screens were the members of her watch, each at a desk/console,

each with a dozen smaller screens to monitor.
Most of the large screens displayed the usual data
from the millions of objects monitored by Nav/
Track radar, cameras, and computers. But fully a
quarter of them now showed curved, empty corridors where nothing moved, or equally lifeless
rooms. In some of them skeletons could be seen.

The three of them faced the largest screen on
Bach's desk, and unconsciously leaned a little
closer as a picture started to form. At first it was
just streaks of color. Klosinski consulted a datapad
on his wrist.

"This is from camera 14/P/delta. It's on the
Promenade Deck. Most of that deck was a sort of
PX, with shopping areas, theaters, clubs, so forth.
But one sector had VIP suites, for when people
visited the station. This one's just outside the
Presidential Suite."

"What's wrong with the picture?"

Klosinski sighed.

"Same thing wrong with all of them. The
cameras are old. We've got about five percent of
them in some sort of working order, which is a
miracle. The Charlie computer is fighting us for
every one."

"I figured it would."

"In just a minute ... there! Did you see it?"

All Bach could see was a stretch of corridor,
maybe a little fancier than some of the views
already up on the wall, but not what Bach
thought of as VIP. She peered at it, but nothing
changed.

"No, nothing's going to happen now. This is a
tape. We got it when the camera first came on."
He fiddled with his datapad, and the screen
resumed its multi-colored static. "I rewound it.
Watch the door on the left."

This time Klosinski stopped the tap on the first recognizable image on the screen.

"This is someone's leg," he said, pointing. "And this is the tail of a dog."

Bach studied it. The leg was bare, and so was the foot. It could be seen from just below the knee.

"That looks like a Sheltie's tail," she said.

"We thought so, too."

"What about the foot?"

"Look at the door," Steiner said. "In relation to the door, the leg looks kind of small."

"You're right," Bach said. A *child?* she wondered. "Okay. Watch this one around the clock. I suppose if there was a camera in that room, you'd have told me about it."

"I guess VIP's don't like to be watched."

"Then carry on as you were. Activate every camera you can, and tape them *all*. I've got to take this to Hoeffer."

She started down out of her well-less office, adjusting her cap at an angle she hoped looked smart and alert.

"Anna," Steiner called. She looked back.

"How did Hoeffer take it when you reminded him Tango Charlie only has six more days left?"

"He threw his pipe at me."

Charlie put Conrad and Helga back in the whelping box, along with Dieter and Inga. All four of them were squealing, which was only natural, but the quality of their squeals changed when Fuchsia jumped in with them, sat down on Dieter, then plopped over on her side. There was nothing that sounded or looked more determined than a blind, hungry, newborn puppy, Charlie thought.

The babies found the swollen nipples, and

Fuchsia fussed over them, licking their little bottoms. Charlie held her breath. It almost looked as if she was counting her brood, and that certainly wouldn't do.

"Good dog, Fuchsia," she cooed, to distract her, and it did. Fuchsia looked up, said I haven't got time for you now, Charlie, and went back to her chores.

"How was the funeral?" asked Tik-Tok the Clock.

"Shut up!" Charlie hissed. "You ... you big idiot! It's okay, Foosh."

Fuchsia was already on her side, letting the pups nurse and more or less ignoring both Charlie and Tik-Tok. Charlie got up and went into the bathroom. She closed and secured the door behind her.

"The funeral was very beautiful," she said, pushing the stool nearer the mammoth marble washbasin and climbing up on it. Behind the basin the whole wall was a mirror, and when she stood on the stool she could see herself. She flounced her blonde hair out and studied it critically. There were some tangles.

"Tell me about it," Tik-Tok said. "I want to know *every* detail."

So she told him, pausing a moment to sniff her armpits. Wearing the suit always made her smell so gross. She clambered up onto the broad marble counter, went around the basin and goosed the 24-karat gold tails of the two dolphins who cavorted there, and water began gushing out of their mouths. She sat with her feet in the basin, touching one tail or another when the water got too hot, and told Tik-Tok all about it.

Charlie used to bathe in the big tub. It was so big it was more suited for swimming laps than bathing. One day she slipped and hit her head and almost drowned. Now she usually bathed in the sink, which was not quite big enough, but a lot safer.

"The rose was the most wonderful part," she said. "I'm glad you thought of that. It just turned and turned and turned ..."

"Did you say anything?"

"I sang a song. A hymn."

"Could I hear it?"

She lowered herself into the basin. Resting the back of her neck on a folded towel, the water came up to her chin, and her legs from the knees down stuck out of the other end. She lowered her mouth a little, and made burbling sounds in the water.

"Can I hear it? I'd like to hear."

"Lord guide and guard all those who fly ..."

Tik-Tok listened to it once, then joined in harmony as she sang it again, and on the third time through added an organ part. Charlie felt the tears in her eyes again, and wiped them with the back of her hand.

"Time to scrubba-scrubba-scrubba," Tik-Tok suggested.

Charlie sat on the edge of the basin with her feet in the water, and lathered a washcloth.

"Scrubba-scrub beside your nose," Tik-Tok sang.

"Scrubba-scrub beside your nose," Charlie repeated, and industriously scoured all around her face.

"Scrubba-scrub between your toes. Scrub all the jelly out of your belly. Scrub your butt, and your you-know-what."

Tik-Tok led her through the ritual she'd been doing so long she didn't even remember how long. A couple times he made her giggle by throwing in a new verse. He was always making them up. When she was done, she was about the cleanest little girl anyone ever saw, except for her hair.

"I'll do that later," she decided, and hopped to the floor, where she danced the drying-off dance in front of the warm air blower until Tik-Tok told her she could stop. Then she crossed the room to the vanity table and sat on the high stool she had installed there.

"Charlie, there's something I wanted to talk to you about," Tik-Tok said.

Charlie opened a tube called "Coral Peaches" and smeared it all over her lips. She gazed at the thousand other bottles and tubes, wondering what she'd use this time.

"Charlie, are you listening to me?"

"Sure," Charlie said. She reached for a bottle labeled "The Glenlivet, Twelve Years Old," twisted the cork out of it, and put it to her lips. She took a big swallow, then another, and wiped her mouth on the back of her arm.

"Holy mackerel! That's real sippin' whiskey!" she shouted, and set the bottle down. She reached for a tin of rouge.

"Some people have been trying to talk to me," Tik-Tok said. "I believe they may have seen Albert, and wondered about him."

Charlie looked up, alarmed—and, doing so, accidentally made a solid streak of rouge from her cheekbone to her chin.

"Do you think they shot at Albert?"

"I don't think so. I think they're just curious."

"Will they hurt me?"

"You never can tell."

Charlie frowned, and used her finger to spread black eyeliner all over her left eyelid. She did the same for the right, then used another jar to draw violet purple frown lines on her forehead. With a thick pencil she outlined her eyebrows.

"What do they want?"

"They're just prying people, Charlie. I thought you ought to know. They'll probably try to talk to you, later."

"Should I talk to them?"

"That's up to you."

Charlie frowned even deeper. Then she picked up the bottle of Scotch and had another belt.

She reached for the Rajah's Ruby and hung it around her neck.

Fully dressed and made up now, Charlie paused to kiss Fuchsia and tell her how beautiful her puppies were, then hurried out to the Promenade Deck.

As she did, the camera on the wall panned down a little, and turned a few degrees on its pivot. That made a noise in the rusty mechanism, and Charlie looked up at it. The speaker beside the camera made a hoarse noise, then did it again. There was a little puff of smoke, and an alert sensor quickly directed a spray of extinguishing gas toward it, then itself gave up the ghost. The speaker said nothing else.

Odd noises were nothing new to Charlie. There were places on the wheel where the clatter of faltering mechanisms behind the walls was so loud you could hardly hear yourself think.

She thought of the snoopy people Tik-Tok had mentioned. That camera was probably just the kind of thing they'd like. So she turned her butt to the camera, bent over, and farted at it.

She went to her mother's room, and sat beside her bed telling her all about little Albert's funeral. When she felt she'd been there long enough she kissed her dry cheek and ran out of the room.

Up one level were the dogs. She went from room to room, letting them out, accompanied by a growing horde of barking jumping Shelties. Each was deliriously happy to see her, as usual, and she had to speak sharply to a few when they kept licking her face. They stopped on command; Charlie's dogs were all good dogs.

When she was done there were seventy-two almost identical dogs yapping and running along with her in a sable-and-white tide. They rushed by another camera with a glowing red light, which panned to follow them up, up, and out of sight around the gentle curve of Tango Charlie.

Bach got off the sidewalk at the 34strasse intersection. She worked her way through the crowds in the shopping arcade, then entered the Intersection-park, where the trees were plastic but the winos sleeping on the benches were real. She was on Level Eight. Up here, 34strasse was taprooms and casinos, second-hand stores, missions, pawn shops, and cheap bordellos. Free-lance whores, naked or in elaborate costumes according to their specialty, eyed her and sometimes propositioned her. Hope springs eternal; these men and women saw her every day on her way home. She waved to a few she had met, though never in a professional capacity.

It was a kilometer and a half to Count Otto Von Zeppelin Residential Corridor. She walked beside the slidewalk. Typically, it operated two days out of seven. Her own quarters were at the end of Count Otto, apartment 80. She palmed the printpad, and went in.

She knew she was lucky to be living in such large quarters on a T/A salary. It was two rooms, plus a large bath and a tiny kitchen. She had grown up in a smaller place, shared by a lot more people. The rent was so low because her bed was only ten meters from an arterial tubeway; the floor vibrated loudly every thirty seconds as the capsules rushed by. It didn't bother her. She had spent her first ten years sleeping within a meter of a regional air-circulation station, just beyond a thin metal apartment wall. It left her with a hearing loss she had been too poor to correct until recently.

For most of her ten years in Otto 80 she had lived alone. Five times, for periods varying from two weeks to six months, she shared with a lover, as she was doing now.

When she came in, Ralph was in the other room. She could hear the steady huffing and puffing as he worked out. Bach went to the bathroom and ran a tub as hot as she could stand it, eased herself in, and stretched out. Her blue paper uniform brief floated to the surface; she skimmed, wadded up, and tossed the soggy mass toward the toilet.

She missed. It had been that sort of day.

She lowered herself until her chin was in the water. Beads of sweat popped out on her forehead. She smiled, and mopped her face with a washcloth.

After a while Ralph appeared in the doorway. She could hear him, but didn't open her eyes.

"I didn't hear you come in," he said.

"Next time I'll bring a brass band."

He just kept breathing heavy, gradually getting it under control. That was her most vivid impression of Ralph, she realized; heavy breathing. That, and lots and lots of sweat. And it was no surprise he had nothing to say. Ralph was oblivious to sarcasm. It made him tiresome, sometimes, but with shoulders like his he didn't need to be witty. Bach opened her eyes and smiled at him.

Luna's low gravity made it hard for all but the

most fanatical to aspire to the muscle mass one could develop on the Earth. The typical Lunarian was taller than Earth-normal, and tended to be thinner.

As a much younger woman Bach had become involved, very much against her better judgment, with an earthling of the species "jock." It hadn't worked out, but she still bore the legacy in a marked preference for beefcake. This doomed her to consorting with only two kinds of men: well-muscled mesomorphs from Earth, and single-minded Lunarians who thought nothing of pumping iron for ten hours a day. Ralph was one of the latter.

There was no rule, so far as Bach could discover, that such specimens had to be mental midgets. That was a stereotype. It also happened, in Ralph's case, to be true. While not actually mentally defective, Ralph Goldstein's idea of a touch intellectual problem was how many kilos to bench press. His spare time was spent brushing his teeth or shaving his chest or looking at pictures of himself in bodybuilding magazines. Bach knew for a fact that Ralph thought the Earth and Sun revolved around Luna.

He had only two real interests; lifting weights, and making love to Anna-Louise Bach. She didn't mind that at all.

Ralph had a swastika tattooed on his penis. Early on, Bach had determined that he had no notion of the history of the symbol; he had seen it in an old film and though it looked nice. It amused her to consider what his ancestors might have thought of the adornment.

He brought a stool close to the tub and sat on it, then stepped on a floor button. The tub was Bach's chief luxury. It did a lot of fun things. Now it lifted her on a long rack until she was half out of the water. Ralph started washing that half. She watched his soapy hands.

"Did you go to the doctor?" he asked her.

"Yeah, I finally did."

"What did he say?"

"Said I have cancer."

"How bad?"

"Real bad. It's going to cost a bundle. I don't know if my insurance will cover it all." She closed her eyes and sighed. It annoyed her to have him be right about something. He had nagged her for months to get her medical check-up.

"Will you get it taken care of tomorrow?"

"No. Ralph, I don't have time tomorrow. Next week, I promise. This thing has come up, but it'll be all over next week, one way or another."

He frowned, but didn't say anything. He didn't have to. The human body, its care and maintenance, was the one subject Ralph knew more about than she did, but even she knew it would be cheaper in the long run to have the work done now.

She felt so lazy he had to help her turn over. Damn, but he was good at this. She had never asked him to do it; he seemed to enjoy it. His strong hands dug into her back and found each sore spot, as if by magic. Presently, it wasn't sore anymore.

"What's this thing that's come up?"

"I ... can't tell you about it. Classified, for now."

He didn't protest, nor did he show surprise, though it was the first time Bach's work had taken her into the realm of secrecy.

It was annoying, really. One of Ralph's charms was that he was a good listener. While he wouldn't understand the technical side of anything, he could sometimes offer surprisingly good advice on personal problems. More often, he showed the knack of synthesizing and expressing things Bach had already known, but had not allowed herself to see.

Well, she could tell him part of it.

"There's this satellite," she began. "Tango Charlie. Have you ever heard of it?"

"That's a funny name for a satellite."

"It's what we call it on the tracking logs. It never really had a name—well, it did, a long time ago, but GWA took it over and turned it into a research facility and an Exec's retreat, and they just let it be known as TC-38. They got it in a war with Telecommunion, part of the peace treaty. They got Charlie, the Bubble, a couple other big wheels.

"The thing about Charlie . . . it's coming down. In about six days, it's going to spread itself all over the Farside. Should be a pretty big bang."

Ralph continued to knead the backs of her legs. It was never a good idea to rush him. He would figure things out in his own way, at his own speed, or he wouldn't figure them out at all.

"Why is it coming down?"

"It's complicated. It's been derelict for a long time. For a while it had the capacity to make course corrections, but it looks like it's run out of reaction mass, or the computer that's supposed to stabilize it isn't working anymore. For a couple of years it hasn't been making corrections."

"Why does it—"

"A Lunar orbit is never stable. There's the Earth tugging on the satellite, the solar wind, mass concentrations of Luna's surface . . . a dozen things that add up, over time. Charlie's in a very eccentric orbit now. Last time it came within a kilometer of the surface. Next time it's gonna miss us by a gnat's whisker, and the time after that, it hits."

Ralph stopped massaging. When Bach glanced at him, she saw he was alarmed. He had just understood that a very large object was about to hit his home planet, and he didn't like the idea.

'Don't worry," Bach said, "there's a surface installation that might get some damage from the debris, but Charlie won't come within a hundred kilometers of any settlements. We got nothing to worry about on that score."

"Then why don't you just ... push it back up ... you know, go up there and do ..." Whatever it is you do, Bach finished for him. He had no real idea what kept a satellite in orbit in the first place, but knew there were people who handled such matters all the time.

There were other questions he might have asked, as well. Why leave Tango Charlie alone all these years? Why not salvage it? Why allow things to get to this point at all?

All those questions brought her back to classified ground.

She sighed, and turned over.

"I wish we could," she said, sincerely. She noted that the swastika was saluting her, and that seemed like a fine idea, so she let him carry her into the bedroom.

And as he made love to her she kept seeing that incredible tide of Shelties with the painted child in the middle.

After the run, ten laps around the Promenade Deck, Charlie led the pack to the Japanese Garden and let them run free through the tall weeds and vegetable patches. Most of the trees in the Garden were dead. The whole place had once been a formal and carefully tended place of meditation. Four men from Tokyo had been employed full time to take care of it. Now the men were buried under the temple gate, the ponds were covered in green scum, the gracefully arched bridge had collapsed, and the flowerbeds were choked with dog turds.

Charlie had to spend part of each morning in the flower beds, feeding Mister Shitface. This was a cylindrical structure with a big round hole in its side, an intake for the wheel's recycling system. It ate dog feces, weeds, dead plants, soil, scraps ... practically anything Charlie shoved into it. The cylinder was painted green, like a frog, and had a face painted on it, with big lips outlining the hole. Charlie sang The Shit-Shoveling Song as she worked.

Tik-Tok had taught her the song, and he used to sing it with her. But a long time ago he had gone deaf in the Japanese Garden. Usually, all Charlie had to do was talk, and Tik-Tok would hear. But there were some places—and more of them every year—where Tik-Tok was deaf.

" '... *Raise dat laig,*' " Charlie puffed. " *'Lif dat tail, If I gets in trouble will you go my bail?*' "

She stopped, and mopped her face with a red bandanna. As usual, there were dogs sitting on the edge of the flowerbed watching Charlie work. Their ears were lifted. They found this *endlessly* fascinating. Charlie just wished it would be over. But you took the bad with the good. She started shoveling again.

" *'I gets weary, O' all dis shovelin'* ...' "

When she was finished she went back on the Promenade.

"What's next?" she asked.

"Plenty," said Tik-Tok. "The funeral put you behind schedule."

He directed her to the infirmary with the new

litter. There they weighed, photographed, X-rayed, and catalogued each puppy. The results were put on file for later registration with the American Kennel Club. It quickly became apparent that Conrad was going to be a cull. He had an overbite. With the others it was too early to tell. She and Tik-Tok would examine them weekly, and their standards were an order of magnitude more stringent than the AKC's. Most of her *culls* would easily have best of breed in a show, and as for her breeding animals ...

"I ought to be able to write Champion on most of these pedigrees."

"You must be patient."

Patient, yeah, she'd heard that before. She took another drink of Scotch. *Champion Fuchsia O'Charlie Station*, she thought. *Now* that *would really make a breeder's day.*

After the puppies, there were two from an earlier litter who were now ready for a final evaluation. Charlie brought them in, and she and Tik-Tok argued long and hard about the points so fine few people would have seen them at all. In the end, they decided both would be sterilized.

Then it was noon feeding. Charlie never enforced discipline here. She let them jump and bark and nip at each other, as long as it didn't get *too* rowdy. She led them all to the cafeteria (and was tracked by three wall cameras), where the troughs of hard kibble and soft soyaburger were already full. Today it was chicken-flavored, Charlie's favorite.

Afternoon was training time. Consulting the records Tik-Tok displayed on a screen, she got the younger dogs one at a time and put each of them through thirty minutes of leash work, up and down the Promenade, teaching them Heel, Sit, Stay, Down, Come according to their degree of progress and Tik-Tok's rigorous schedules. The older dogs were taken to the Ring in groups, where they sat obediently in a line as she put them, one by one, through free-heeling paces.

Finally it was evening meals, which she hated. It was all human food.

"Eat your vegetables," Tik-Tok would say. "Clean up your plate. People are starving in New Dresden." It was usually green salads and yucky broccoli and beets and stuff like that. Tonight it was yellow squash, which Charlie liked about as much as a root canal. She gobbled up the hamburger patty and then dawdled over the squash until it was a yellowish mess all over her plate like baby shit. Half of it ended up on the table. Finally Tik-Tok relented and let her get back to her duties, which, in the evening, was grooming. She brushed each dog until the coats shone. Some of the dogs had already settled in for the night, and she had to wake them up.

At last, yawning, she made her way back to her room. She was pretty well plastered by then. Tik-Tok, who was used to it, made allowances and tried to jolly her out of what seemed a very black mood.

"There's *nothing* wrong!" she shouted at one point, tears streaming from her eyes. Charlie could be an ugly drunk.

She staggered out to the Promenade Deck and lurched from wall to wall, but she never fell down. Ugly or not, she knew how to hold her liquor. It had been ages since it made her sick.

The elevator was in what had been a commercial zone. The empty shops gaped at her as she punched the button. She took another drink, and the door opened. She got in.

She hated this part. The elevator was rising up through a spoke, toward the hub of the wheel.

She got lighter as the car went up, and the trip did funny things to the inner ear. She hung on to the hand rail until the car shuddered to a stop.

Now everything was fine. She was almost weightless up here. Weightlessness was great when you were drunk. When there was no gravity to worry about, your head didn't spin—and if it did, it didn't matter.

This was one part of the wheel where the dogs never went. They could never get used to falling, no matter how long they were kept up here. But Charlie was an expert in falling. When she got the blues she came up here and pressed her face to the huge ballroom window.

People were only a vague memory to Charlie. Her mother didn't count. Though she visited every day, mom was about as lively as V.I. Lenin. Sometimes Charlie wanted to be held so much it hurt. The dogs were good, they were warm, they licked her, they loved her . . . but they couldn't hold her.

Tears leaked from her eyes, which was really a bitch in the ballroom, because tears could get *huge* in here. She wiped them away and looked out the window.

The moon was getting bigger again. She wondered what it meant. Maybe she would ask Tik-Tok.

She made it back as far as the Garden. Inside, the dogs were sleeping in a huddle. She knew she ought to get them back to their rooms, but she was far too drunk for that. And Tik-Tok couldn't do a damn thing about it in here. He couldn't see, and he couldn't hear.

She lay down on the ground, curled up, and was asleep in seconds.

When she started to snore, the three or four

dogs who had come over to watch her sleep licked her mouth until she stopped. Then they curled up beside her. Soon they were joined by others, until she slept in the middle of a blanket of dogs.

A crisis team had been assembled in the monitoring room when Bach arrived the next morning. They seemed to have been selected by Captain Hoeffer, and there were so many of them that there was not enough room for everyone to sit down. Bach led them to a conference room just down the hall, and everyone took seats around the long table. Each seat was equipped with a computer display, and there was a large screen on the wall behind Hoeffer, at the head of the table. Bach took her place on his right, and across from her was Deputy Chief Zeiss, a man with a good reputation in the department. He made Bach very nervous. Hoeffer, on the other hand, seemed to relish his role. Since Zeiss seemed content to be an observer, Bach decided to sit back and speak only if called upon.

Noting that every seat was filled, and that what she assumed were assistants had pulled up chairs behind their principles, Bach wondered if this many people were really required for this project. Steiner, sitting at Bach's right, leaned over and spoke quietly.

"Pick a time," he said.

"What's that?"

"I said pick a time. We're running an office pool. If you come closest to the time security is broken, you win a hundred Marks."

"Is ten minutes from now spoken for?"

They quieted when Hoeffer stood up to speak.

"Some of you have been working on this problem all night," he said. "Others have been called in to give us your expertise in the matter. I'd like to welcome Deputy Chief Zeiss, representing the Mayor and the Chief of Police. Chief Zeiss, would you like to say a few words?"

Zeiss merely shook his hand, which seemed to surprise Hoeffer. Bach knew he would never have passed up an opportunity like that, and probably couldn't understand how anyone else could.

"Very well. We can start with Doctor Blume."

Blume was a sour little man who affected wire-rimmed glasses and a cheap toupee over what must have been a completely bald head. Bach thought it odd that a medical man would wear such clumsy prosthetics, calling attention to problems that were no harder to cure than a hangnail. She idly called up his profile on her screen, and was surprised to learn he had a Nobel Prize.

"The subject is a female caucasoid, almost certainly Earthborn."

On the wall behind Hoeffer and on Bach's screen, tapes of the little girl and her dogs were being run.

"She displays no obvious abnormalities. In several shots she is nude, and clearly has not yet reached puberty. I estimate her age between seven and ten years old. There are small discrepancies in her behavior. Her movements are economical—except when playing. She accomplishes various hand-eye tasks with a maturity beyond her apparent years." The doctor sat down abruptly.

It put Hoeffer off balance.

"Ah . . . that's fine, doctor. But, if you recall, I just asked you to tell me how old she is, and if she's healthy."

"She appears to be eight. I said that."

"Yes, but—"

"What do you want from me?" Blume said, suddenly angry. He glared around at many of the assembled experts. "There's something badly wrong with that girl. I say she is eight. Fine! Any fool could see that. I say I can observe no health problems visually. For this, you need a doctor? Bring her to me, give me a few days, and I'll give you six volumes on her health. But video-tapes . . . ?" He trailed off, his silence as eloquent as his words.

"Thank you, Doctor Blume," Hoeffer said. "As soon as—"

"I'll tell you one thing, though," Blume said, in a low, dangerous tone. "It is a disgrace to let that child drink liquor like that. The effects in later life will be terrible. I have seen large men in their thirties and forties who could not hold half as much as I saw her drink . . . *in one day!*" He glowered at Hoeffer for a moment. "I was sworn to silence. But I want to know who is responsible for this."

Bach realized he didn't know where the girl was. She wondered how many of the others in the room had been filled in, and how many were working only on their own part of the problem.

"It will be explained," Zeiss said, quietly. Blume looked from Zeiss to Hoeffer, and back, then settled into his chair, not mollified but willing to wait.

"Thank you, Doctor Blume," Hoeffer said again. "Next we'll hear from . . . Ludmilla Rossnikova, representing the GMA Conglomerate."

Terrific, thought Bach. He's brought GMA into it. No doubt he swore Ms. Rossnikova to secrecy, and if he really thought she would fail to mention it to her supervisor then he was even dumber than Bach had thought. She had worked for them once, long ago, and though she was just an employee she had learned something about them. GMA had its roots deep in twentieth-century Japanese industry. When you went to work on the executive level at GMA, you were set up for life. They expected, and received, loyalty that compared favorably with that demanded by the Mafia. Which meant that, by telling Rossnikova his "secret," Hoeffer had insured that three hundred GMA execs knew about it three minutes later. They could be relied on to keep a secret, but only if it benefited GMA.

"The computer on Tango Charlie was a custom-designed array," Rossnikova began. "That was the usual practice in those days, with BioLogic computers. It was designated the same as the station: BioLogic TC-38. It was one of the largest installations of its time.

"At the time of the disaster, when it was clear that everything had failed, the TC-38 was given its final instructions. Because of the danger, it was instructed to impose an interdiction zone around the station, which you'll find described under the label Interdiction on your screens."

Rossnikova paused while many of those present called up this information.

"To implement the zone, the TC-38 was given command of certain defensive weapons. These included ten bevawatt lasers ... and other weapons which I have not been authorized to name or describe, other than to say they are at least as formidable as the lasers."

Hoeffer looked annoyed, and was about to say something, but Zeiss stopped him with a gesture. Each understood that the lasers were enough in themselves.

"So while it is possible to destroy the station," Rossnikova went on, "there is no chance of boarding it—assuming anyone would even want to try."

Bach thought she could tell from the different expressions around the table which people knew the whole story and which knew only their part of it. A couple of the latter seemed ready to ask a question, but Hoeffer spoke first.

"How about canceling the computer's instructions?" he said. "Have you tried that?"

"That's been tried many times over the last few years, as this crisis got closer. We didn't expect it to work, and it did not. Tango Charlie won't accept a new program."

"Oh my God," Doctor Blume gasped. Bach saw that his normally florid face had paled. "Tango Charlie. She's on Tango Charlie."

"That's right, doctor," said Hoeffer. "And we're trying to figure out how to get her off. Doctor Wilhelm?"

Wilhelm was an older woman with the stocky build of the Earthborn. She rose, and looked down at some notes in her hand.

"Information's under the label Neurotropic Agent X on your machines," she muttered, then looked up at them. "But you needn't bother. That's about as far as we got, naming it. I'll sum up what we know, but you don't need an expert for this; there *are* no experts on Neuro-X.

"It broke out on August 9, thirty years ago next month. The initial report was five cases, one death. Symptoms were progressive paralysis, convulsions, loss of motor control, numbness.

"Tango Charlie was immediately quarantined as a standard procedure. An epidemiological team was dispatched from Atlanta, followed by another from New Dresden. All ships which had left Tango Charlie were ordered to return, except for one on its way to Mars and another already in parking orbit around Earth. The one in Earth orbit was forbidden to land.

"By the time the teams arrived, there were over a hundred reported cases, and six more deaths. Later symptoms included blindness and deafness. It progressed at different rates in different people, but it was always quite fast. Mean survival time from onset of symptoms was later determined to be forty-eight hours. Nobody lived longer than four days.

"Both medical teams immediately came down with it, as did a third, and a fourth team. *All* of them came down with it, each and every person. The first two teams had been using class three isolation techniques. It didn't matter. The third team stepped up the precautions to class two. Same result. Very quickly we had been forced into class one procedures—which involves isolation as total as we can get it: no physical contact whatsoever, no sharing of air supplies, all air to the investigators filtered through a sterilizing environment. They *still* got it. Six patients and some tissue samples were sent to a class one installation two hundred miles from New Dresden, and more patients were sent, with class one precautions, to a hospital ship close to Charlie. Everyone at both facilities came down with it. We *almost* sent a couple of patients to Atlanta."

She paused, looking down and rubbing her forehead. No one said anything.

"I was in charge," she said, quietly. "I can't take credit for not shipping anyone to Atlanta. We were going to . . . and suddenly there wasn't anybody left on Charlie to load patients aboard. All dead or dying.

"We backed off. Bear in mind this all happened in five days. What we had to show for those five days was a major space station with all aboard dead, three ships full of dead people, and an epidemiological research facility here on Luna full of dead people.

"After that, politicians began making most of the decisions—but I advised them. The two nearby ships were landed by robot control at the infected research station. The derelict ship going to Mars was ... I think it's still classified, but what the hell? It was blown up with a nuclear weapon. Then we started looking into what was left. The station here was easiest. There was one cardinal rule: *nothing* that went into that station was to come out. Robot crawlers brought in remote manipulators and experimental animals. Most of the animals died. Neuro-X killed most mammals: monkeys, rats, cats—"

"Dogs?" Bach asked. Wilhelm glanced at her.

"It didn't kill *all* the dogs. Half of the ones we sent in lived."

"Did you know that there were dogs alive on Charlie?"

"No. The interdiction was already set up by then. Charlie Station was impossible to land, and too close and too visible to nuke, because that would violate about a dozen corporate treaties. And there seemed no reason not to just leave it there. We had our samples isolated here at the Lunar station. We decided to work with that, and forget about Charlie."

"Thank you, doctor."

"As I was saying, it was by far the most virulent organism we had ever seen. It seemed to have a taste for all sorts of neural tissue, in almost every mammal.

"The teams that went in never had time to learn anything. They were all disabled too quickly, and just as quickly they were dead. We didn't find out much, either ... for a variety of reasons.

My guess is it was a virus, simply because we would certainly have seen anything larger almost immediately. But we never *did* see it. It was fast getting in—we don't know how it was vectored, but the only reliable shield was several miles of vacuum—and once it got in, I suspect it worked changes on genetic material of the host, setting up a secondary agent which I'm almost sure we isolated ... and then it went away and hid very well. It was still in the host, in some form, it *had* to be, but we think its active life in the nervous system was on the order of one hour. But by then it had already done its damage. It set the system against itself, and the host was consumed in about two days."

Wilhelm had grown increasingly animated. A few times Bach thought she was about to get incoherent. It was clear the nightmare of Neuro-X had not diminished for her with the passage of thirty years. But now she made an effort to slow down again.

"The other remarkable thing about it was, of course, its infectiousness. Nothing I've ever seen was so persistent in evading our best attempts at keeping it isolated. Add that to its mortality rate, which, at the time, seemed to be one hundred percent ... and you have the second great reason why we learned so little about it."

"What was the first?" Hoeffer asked. Wilhelm glared at him.

"The difficulty of investigating such a subtle process of infection by remote control."

"Ah, of course."

"The other thing was simply fear. Too many people had died for there to be any hope of hushing it up. I don't know if anyone tried. I'm sure those of you who were old enough remember the uproar. So the public debate was loud and long, and the pressure for extreme measures was intense . . . and, I should add, not unjustified. The argument was simple. Everyone who got it was dead. I believe that if those patients had been sent to Atlanta, everyone on *Earth* would have died. Therefore . . . what was the point of taking a chance by keeping it alive and studying it?"

Doctor Blume cleared his throat, and Wilhelm looked at him.

"As I recall, doctor," he said, "there were two reasons raised. One was the abstract one of scientific knowledge. Though there might be no point in studying Neuro-X since no one was afflicted with it, we might learn something by the study itself."

"Point taken," Wilhelm said, "and no argument."

"And the second was, we never found out where Neuro-X came from . . . there were rumors it was a biological warfare agent." He looked at Rossnikova, as if asking her what comment GMA might want to make about *that*. Rossnikova said nothing. "But most people felt it was a spontaneous mutation. There have been several instances of that in the high-radiation environment of a space station. And if it happened once, what's to prevent it from happening again?"

"Again, you'll get no argument from me. In fact, I supported both those positions when the question was being debated." Wilhelm grimaced, then looked right at Blume. "But the fact is, I didn't support them very hard, and when the Lunar station was sterilized, I felt a lot better."

Blume was nodding.

"I'll admit it. I felt better, too."

"And if Neuro-X were to show up again," she went on, quietly, "my advice would be to sterilize immediately. Even if it meant losing a city."

Blume said nothing. Bach watched them both

for a while in the resulting silence, finally, understanding just how much Wilhelm feared this thing.

There was a lot more. The meeting went on for three hours, and everyone got a chance to speak. Eventually, the problem was outlined to everyone's satisfaction.

Tango Charlie could not be boarded. It could be destroyed. (Some time was spent debating the wisdom of the original interdiction order—beating a dead horse, as far as Bach was concerned—and questioning whether it might be possible to countermand it.)

But things could *leave* Tango Charlie. It would only be necessary to withdraw the robot probes that had watched so long and faithfully, and the survivors could be evacuated.

That left the main question. *Should* they be evacuated?

(The fact that only one survivor had been sighted so far was not mentioned. Everyone assumed others would show up sooner or later. After all, it was simply not possible that just one eight-year-old girl could be the only occupant of a station no one had entered or left for thirty years.)

Wilhelm, obviously upset but clinging strongly to her position, advocated blowing up the station at once. There was some support for this, but only about ten percent of the group.

The eventual decision, which Bach had predicted before the meeting even started, was to do nothing at the moment.

After all, there were almost five whole days to keep thinking about it.

"There's a call waiting for you," Steiner said,

when she got back to the monitoring room. "The switchboard says it's important."

Bach went into her office—wishing yet again for one with walls—flipped a switch.

"Bach," she said. Nothing came on the vision screen.

"I'm curious," said a woman's voice. "Is this the Anna-Louise Bach who worked in The Bubble ten years ago?"

For a moment, Bach was too surprised to speak, but she felt a wave of heat as blood rushed to her face. She knew the voice.

"Hello? Are you there?"

"Why no vision?" she asked.

"First, are you alone? And is your instrument secure?"

"The instrument is secure, if yours is." Bach flipped another switch, and a privacy hood descended around her screen. The sounds of the room faded as a sonic scrambler began operating. "And I'm alone."

Megan Galloway's face appeared on the screen. One part of Bach's mind noted that she hadn't changed much, except that her hair was curly and red.

"I thought you might not wish to be seen with me," Galloway said. Then she smiled. "Hello, Anna-Louise. How are you?"

"I don't think it really matters if I'm seen with you," Bach said.

"No? Then would you care to comment on why the New Dresden Police Department, among other government agencies, is allowing an eight-year-old child to go without the rescue she so obviously needs?"

Bach said nothing.

"Would you comment on the rumor that the NDPD does not intend to effect the child's rescue?

That, if it can get away with it, the NDPD will let the child be smashed to pieces?"

Still Bach waited.

Galloway sighed, and ran a hand through her hair.

"You're the most exasperating woman I've ever known, Bach," she said. "Listen, don't you even want to try to talk me out of going with the story?"

Bach almost said something, but decided to wait once more.

"If you want to, you can meet me at the end of your shift. The Mozartplatz. I'm on the *Great Northern*, suite 1, but I'll see you in the bar on the top deck."

"I'll be there," Bach said, and broke the connection.

Charlie sang the Hangover Song most of the morning. It was not one of her favorites.

There was penance to do, of course. Tik-Tok made her drink a foul glop that—she had to admit—did do wonders for her headache. When she was done she was drenched in sweat, but her hangover was gone.

"You're lucky," Tik-Tok said. "Your hangovers are never severe."

"They're severe enough for me," Charlie said.

He made her wash her hair, too.

After that, she spent some time with her mother. She always valued that time. Tik-Tok was a good friend, mostly, but he was so *bossy*. Charlie's mother never shouted at her, never scolded or lectured. She simply listened. True, she wasn't very active. But it was nice to have somebody just to talk to. One day, Charlie hoped, her mother would walk again. Tik-Tok said that was unlikely.

Then she had to round up the dogs and take them for their morning run.

And everywhere she went, the red camera eyes followed her. Finally she had enough. She stopped, put her fists on her hips, and shouted at a camera.

"You stop that!" she said.

The camera started to make noises. At first she couldn't understand anything, then some words started to come through.

"... *lie, Tango ... Foxtrot ... in, please. Tango Charlie ...*"

"Hey, that's my name."

The camera continued to buzz and spit noise at her.

"Tik-Tok, is that you?"

"I'm afraid not, Charlie."

"What's going on, then?"

"It's those nosy people. They've been watching you, and now they're trying to talk to you. But I'm holding them off. I don't think they'll bother you, if you just ignore the cameras."

"But why are you fighting them?"

"I didn't think you'd want to be bothered."

Maybe there was some of that hangover still around. Anyway, Charlie got real angry at Tik-Tok, and called him some names he didn't approve of. She knew she'd pay for it later, but for now Tik-Tok was pissed, and in no mood to reason with her. So he let her have what she wanted, on the principle that getting what you want is usually the worst thing that can happen to anybody.

"*Tango Charlie, this is Foxtrot Romeo. Come in, please. Tango—*"

"Come in *where?*" Charlie asked, reasonably. "And my name isn't Tango."

* * *

Bach was so surprised to have the little girl actually reply that for a moment she couldn't think of anything to say.

"Uh ... it's just an expression," Bach said. "Come in ... that's radio talk for 'please answer.'"

"Then you should say please answer," the little girl pointed out.

"Maybe you're right. My name is Bach. You can call me Anna-Louise, if you'd like. We've been trying to—"

"Why should I?"

"Excuse me?"

"Excuse you for what?"

Bach looked at the screen and drummed her fingers silently for a short time. Around her in the monitoring room, there was not a sound to be heard. At last, she managed a smile.

"Maybe we started off on the wrong foot."

"Which foot would that be?"

The little girl just kept staring at her. Her expression was not amused, not hostile, not really argumentative. Then why was the conversation suddenly so maddening?

"Could I make a statement?" Bach tried.

"I don't know. Can you?"

Bach's fingers didn't tap this time; they were balled up in a fist. "I shall, anyway. My name is Anna-Louise Bach. I'm talking to you from New Dresden, Luna. That's a city on the moon, which you can probably see—"

"I know where it is."

"Fine. I've been trying to contact you for many hours, but your computer has been fighting me all the time."

"That's right. He said so."

"Now, I can't explain why he's been fighting me, but—"

"I know why. He thinks you're nosy."

"I won't deny that. But we're trying to help you."

"Why?"

"Because ... it's what we do. Now if you could—"

"Hey. Shut up, will you?"

Bach did so. With forty-five other people at their scattered screens, Bach watched the little girl—the *horrible* little girl, as she was beginning to think of her—take a long pull from the green glass bottle of Scotch whiskey. She belched, wiped her mouth with the back of her hand, and scratched between her legs. When she was done, she smelled her fingers.

She seemed about to say something, then cocked her head, listening to something Bach couldn't hear.

"That's a good idea," she said, then got up and ran away. She was just vanishing around the curve of the deck when Hoeffer burst into the room, trailed by six members of his advisory team. Bach leaned back in her chair, and tried to fend off thoughts of homicide.

"I was told you'd established contact," Hoeffer said, leaning over Bach's shoulder in a way she absolutely *detested*. He peered at the lifeless scene. "What happened to her?"

"I don't know. She said, 'That's a good idea,' got up, and ran off."

"I told you to keep her here until I got a chance to talk to her."

"I tried," Bach said.

"You should have—"

"I have her on camera nineteen," Steiner called out.

Everyone watched as the technicians followed the girl's progress on the working cameras. They saw her enter a room to emerge in a moment

with a big-screen monitor. Bach tried to call her
each time she passed a camera, but it seemed
only the first one was working for incoming calls.
She passed through the range of four cameras
before coming back to the original, where she
carefully unrolled the monitor and tacked it to
the wall, then payed out the cord and plugged it
in very close to the wall camera Bach's team had
been using. She unshipped this camera from its
mount. The picture jerked around for awhile, and
finally steadied. The girl had set it on the floor.

"Stabilize that," Bach told her team, and the
picture on her monitor righted itself. She now
had a worm's-eye view of the corridor. The girl
sat down in front of the camera, and grinned.

"Now I can see you," she said. Then she
frowned. "If you send me a picture."

"Bring a camera over here," Bach ordered.

While it was being set up, Hoeffer shouldered
her out of the way and sat in her chair.

"There you are," the girl said. And again, she
frowned. "That's funny. I was sure you were a
girl. Did somebody cut your balls off?"

Now it was Hoeffer's turn to be speechless.
There were a few badly suppressed giggles; Bach
quickly silenced them with her most ferocious
glare, while giving thanks no one would ever
know how close she had come to bursting into
laughter.

"Never mind that," Hoeffer said. "My name is
Hoeffer. Would you go get your parents? We need
to talk to them."

"No," said the girl. "And no."

"What's that?"

"No, I won't get them," the girl clarified, "and
no, you don't need to talk to them."

Hoeffer had little experience dealing with
children.

"Now, please be reasonable," he began, in a wheedling tone. "We're trying to help you, after all. We have to talk to your parents, to find out more about your situation. After that, we're going to help you get out of there."

"I want to talk to the lady," the girl said.

"She's not here."

"I think you're lying. She talked to me just a minute ago."

"I'm in charge."

"In charge of what?"

"Just in charge. Now, go get your parents!"

They all watched as she got up and moved closer to the camera. All they could see at first was her feet. Then water began to splash on the lens.

Nothing could stop the laughter this time, as Charlie urinated on the camera.

For three hours Bach watched the screens. Every time the girl passed the prime camera Bach called out to her. She had thought about it carefully. Bach, like Hoeffer, did not know a lot about children. She consulted briefly with the child psychologist on Hoeffer's team and the two of them outlined a tentative game plan. The guy seemed to know what he was talking about and, even better, his suggestions agreed with what Bach's common sense told her should work.

So she never said anything that might sound like an order. While Hoeffer seethed in the background, Bach spoke quietly and reasonably every time the child showed up. "I'm still here," she would say. "We could talk," was a gentle suggestion. "You want to play?"

She longed to use one line the psychologist suggested, one that would put Bach and the child on the same team, so to speak. The line was "The idiot's gone. You want to talk now?"

Eventually the girl began glancing at the camera. She had a different dog every time she came by. At first Bach didn't realize this, as they were almost completely identical. Then she noticed they came in slightly different sizes.

"That's a beautiful dog," she said. The girl looked up, then started away. "I'd like to have a dog like that. What's its name?"

"This is Madam's Sweet Brown Sideburns, Say *hi*, Brownie." The dog yipped. "Sit up for mommy, Brownie. Now roll over. Stand tall. Now go in a circle, Brownie, that's a good doggy, walk on your hind legs. Now *jump*, Brownie. Jump, jump, *jump!*" The dog did exactly as he was told, leaping into the air and turning a flip each time the girl commanded it. Then he sat down, pink tongue hanging out, eyes riveted on his master.

"I'm impressed," Bach said, and it was the literal truth. Like other citizens of Luna, Bach had never seen a wild animal, had never owned a pet, knew animals only from the municipal zoo, where care was taken not to interfere with natural behaviors. She had had no idea animals could be so smart, and no inkling of how much work had gone into the exhibition she had just seen.

"It's nothing," the girl said. "You should see his father. Is this Anna-Louise again?"

"Yes, it is. What's your name?"

"Charlie. You ask a lot of questions."

"I guess I do. I just want to—"

"I'd like to ask some questions, too."

"All right. Go ahead."

"I have six of them, to start off with. One, why should I call you Anna-Louise? Two, why should I excuse you? Three, what is the wrong foot? Four ... but that's not a question, really, since you already proved you *can* make a statement, if you wish, by doing so. Four, why are you trying to help me? Five, why do you want to see my parents?''

It took Bach a moment to realize that these were the questions Charlie had asked in their first, maddening conversation, questions she had not gotten answers for. And they were in their original order.

And they didn't make a hell of a lot of sense.

But the child psychologist was making motions with his hands, and nodding his encouragement to Bach, so she started in.

"You should call me Anna-Louise because ... it's my first name, and friends call each other by their first names.''

"Are we friends?''

"Well, I'd like to be your friend.''

"Why?''

"Look, you don't have to call me Anna-Louise if you don't want to.''

"I don't mind. Do I have to be your friend?''

"Not if you don't want to.''

"Why should I want to?''

And it went on like that. Each question spawned a dozen more, and a further dozen sprang from each of those. Bach had figured to get Charlie's six—make that five—questions out of the way quickly, then get to the important things. She soon began to think she'd never answer even the *first* question.

She was involved in a long and awkward explanation of friendship, going over the ground for the tenth time, when words appeared at the bottom of her screen.

Put your foot down, they said. She glanced up at the child psychologist. He was nodding, but making quieting gestures with his hands. "But gently," the man whispered.

Right, Bach thought. Put your foot down. And get off on the wrong foot again.

"That's enough of that," Bach said abruptly.

"Why?" asked Charlie.

"Because I'm tired of that. I want to do something else."

"All right," Charlie said. Bach saw Hoeffer waving frantically, just out of camera range.

"Uh . . . Captain Hoeffer is still here. He'd like to talk to you."

"That's just too bad for him. I don't want to talk to him."

Good for you, Bach thought. But Hoeffer was still waving.

"Why not? He's not so bad." Bach felt ill, but avoided showing it.

"He lied to me. He said you'd gone away."

"Well, he's in charge here, so—"

"I'm warning you," Charlie said, and waited a dramatic moment, shaking her finger at the screen. "You put that poo-poo-head back on, and I won't come in ever again."

Bach looked helplessly at Hoeffer, who at last nodded.

"I want to talk about dogs," Charlie announced.

So that's what they did for the next hour. Bach was thankful she had studied up on the subject when the dead puppy first appeared. Even so, there was no doubt as to who was the authority. Charlie knew everything there was to know about dogs. And of all the experts Hoeffer had called in, not one could tell Bach anything about the goddamn animals. She wrote a note and handed it to Steiner, who went off to find a zoologist.

Finally Bach was able to steer the conversation around to Charlie's parents.

"My father is dead," Charlie admitted.

"I'm sorry," Bach said. "When did he die?"

"Oh, a long time ago. He was a spaceship pilot, and one day he went off in his spaceship and never came back." For a moment she looked far away. Then she shrugged. "I was real young."

Fantasy, the psychologist wrote at the bottom of her screen, but Bach had already figured that out. Since Charlie had to have been born many years after the Charlie Station Plague, her father could not have flown any spaceships.

"What about your mother?"

Charlie was silent for a long time, and Bach began to wonder if she was losing contact with her. At last, she looked up.

"You want to talk to my mother?"

"I'd like that very much."

"Okay. But that's all for today. I've got work to do. You've already put me way behind."

"Just bring your mother here, and I'll talk to her, and you can do your work."

"No. I can't do that. But I'll take you to her. Then I'll work, and I'll talk to you tomorrow."

Bach started to protest that tomorrow was not soon enough, but Charlie was not listening. The camera was picked up, and the picture bounced around as she carried it with her. All Bach could see was a very unsteady upside-down view of the corridor.

"She's going into Room 350," said Steiner. "She's been in there twice, and she stayed a while both times."

Bach said nothing. The camera jerked wildly for a moment, then steadied.

"This is my mother," Charlie said. "Mother, this is my friend, Anna-Louise."

The Mozartplatz had not existed when Bach

was a child. Construction on it had begun when
she was five, and the first phase was finished
when she was fifteen. Tenants had begun moving
in soon after that. During each succeeding year
new sectors had been opened, and though a
structure as large as the Mozartplatz would never
be finished—two major sectors were currently
under renovation—it had been essentially completed six years ago.

It was a virtual copy of the Soleri-class arcology
atriums that had sprouted like mushrooms on the
Earth in the last four decades, with the exception
that on Earth you built up, and on Luna you
went down.

First dig a trench fifteen miles long and two
miles deep. Vary the width of the trench, but
never let it get narrower than one mile, nor
broader than five. In some places make the base
of the trench wider than the top, so the walls of
rock loom outward. Now put a roof over it, fill it
with air, and start boring tunnels into the sides.
Turn those tunnels into apartments and shops
and everything else humans need in a city. You
end up with dizzying vistas, endless terraces that
reach higher than the eye can see, a madness of
light and motion and spaces too wide to echo.

Do all that, and you still wouldn't have the
Mozartplatz. To approach that ridiculous level of
grandeur there were still a lot of details to attend
to. Build four mile-high skyscrapers to use as
table legs to support the mid-air golf course.
Crisscross the open space with bridges having no
visible means of support, and encrusted with
shops and homes that cling like barnacles. Sus-
pend apartment buildings from silver balloons
that rise half the day and descend the other half,
reachable only by glider. Put in a fountain with
more water than Niagara, and a ski slope on a

huge spiral ramp. Dig a ten-mile lake in the middle, with a bustling port at each end for the luxury ships that ply back and forth, attach runways to balconies so residents can fly to their front door, stud the interior with zeppelin ports and railway stations and hanging gardens ... and you still don't have Mozartplatz, but you're getting closer.

The upper, older parts of New Dresden, the parts she had grown up in, were spartan and claustrophobic. Long before her time Lunarians had begun to build larger when they could afford it. The newer, lower parts of the city were studded with downscale versions of Mozartplatz, open spaces half a mile wide and maybe fifty levels deep. This was just a logical extension.

She felt she ought to dislike it because it was so overdone, so fantastically huge, such a waste of space ... and, oddly, so standardized. It was a taste of the culture of old Earth, where Paris looked just like Tokyo. She had been to the new Beethovenplatz at Clavius, and it looked just like this place. Six more arco-malls were being built in other Lunar cities.

And Bach liked it. She couldn't help herself. One day she'd like to live here.

She left her tube capsule in the bustling central station, went to a terminal and queried the location of the *Great Northern*. It was docked at the southern port, five miles away.

It was claimed that any form of non-animal transportation humans had ever used was available in the Mozartplatz. Bach didn't doubt it. She had tried most of them. But when she had a little time, as she did today, she liked to walk. She didn't have time to walk five miles, but compromised by walking to the trolley station a mile away.

Starting out on a brick walkway, she moved to cool marble, then over a glass bridge with lights flashing down inside. This took her to a board-walk, then down to a beach where machines made four-foot breakers, each carrying a new load of surfers. The sand was fine and hot between her toes. Mozartplatz was a sensual delight for the feet. Few Lunarians ever wore shoes, and they could walk all day through old New Dresden and feel nothing but different types of carpeting and composition flooring.

The one thing Bach didn't like about the place was the weather. She thought it was needless, preposterous, and inconvenient. It began to rain and, as usual, caught her off guard. She hurried to a shelter where, for a tenthMark, she rented an umbrella, but it was too late for her paper uniform. As she stood in front of a blower, drying off, she wadded it up and threw it away, then hurried to catch the trolley, nude but for her creaking leather equipment belt and police cap. Even this stripped down, she was more dressed than a quarter of the people around her.

The conductor gave her a paper mat to put on the artificial leather seat. There were cut flowers in crystal vases attached to the sides of the car. Bach sat by an open window and leaned one arm outside in the cool breeze, watching the passing scenery. She craned her neck when the *Graf Zeppelin* muttered by overhead. They said it was an exact copy of the first world-girdling dirigible, and she had no reason to doubt it.

It was a great day to be traveling. If not for one thing, it would be perfect. Her mind kept coming back to Charlie and her mother.

She had forgotten just how big the *Great Northern* was. She stopped twice on her way down the long dock to board it, once to buy a lime sherbet ice cream cone, and again to purchase a skirt. As she fed coins into the clothing machine, she looked at the great metal wall of the ship. It was painted white, trimmed in gold. There were five smokestacks and six towering masts. Midships was the housing for the huge paddlewheel. Multi-colored pennants snapped in the breeze from the forest of rigging. It was quite a boat.

She finished her cone, punched in her size, then selected a simple above-the-knee skirt in a gaudy print of tropical fruit and palm trees. The machine hummed as it cut the paper to size, hemmed it and strengthened the waist with elastic, then rolled it out into her hand. She held it up against herself, it was good, but the equipment belt spoiled it.

There were lockers along the deck. She used yet another coin to rent one. In it went the belt and cap. She took the pin out of her hair and shook it down around her shoulders, fussed with it for a moment, then decided it would have to do. She fastened the skirt with its single button, wearing it low on her hips, south-seas style. She walked a few steps, studying the effect. The skirt tended to leave one leg bare when she walked, which felt right.

"Look at you," she chided herself, under her breath. "You think you look all right to meet a worlds-famous, glamorous tube personality? Who you happen to despise?" She thought about reclaiming her belt, then decided that would be foolish. The fact was it was a glorous day, a beautiful ship, and she was feeling more alive than she had in months.

She climbed the gangplank and was met at the top by a man in an outlandish uniform. It was all white, covered everything but his face, and was festooned with gold braid and black buttons. It looked hideously uncomfortable, but he didn't seem to mind it. That was one of the odd things about Mozartplatz. In jobs at places like the *Great Northern*, people often worked in period costumes, though it meant wearing shoes or things even more grotesque.

He made a small bow and tipped his hat, then offered her a hibiscus, which he helped her pin in her hair. She smiled at him. Bach was a sucker for that kind of treatment—and knew it—perhaps because she got so little of it.

"I'm meeting someone in the bar on the top deck."

"If madame would walk this way ..." He gestured, then led her along the side rail toward the stern of the ship. The deck underfoot was gleaming, polished teak.

She was shown to a wicker table near the rail. The steward held the chair out for her, and took her order. She relaxed, looking up at the vast reaches of the arco-mall, feeling the bright sunlight washing over her body, smelling the salt water, hearing the lap of waves against wood pilings. The air was full of bright balloons, gliders, putt-putting nano-lights, and people in muscle-powered flight harnesses. Not too far away, a fish broke the surface. She grinned at it.

Her drink arrived, with sprigs of mint and several straws and a tiny parasol. It was good. She looked around. There were only a few people out here on the deck. One couple was dressed in full period costume, but the rest looked normal enough. She settled on one guy sitting alone across the deck. He had a good pair of shoulders on him. When she caught his eye, she made a hand signal that meant "I might be available." He ignored it, which annoyed her for a while, until he was joined by a tiny woman who couldn't have been five feet tall. She shrugged. No accounting for taste.

She knew what was happening to her. It was silly, but she felt like going on the hunt. It often happened to her when something shocking or unpleasant happened at work. The police headshrinker said it was compensation, and not that uncommon.

With a sigh, she turned her mind away from that. It seemed there was no place else for it to go but back into that room on Charlie Station, and to the thing in the bed.

Charlie knew her mother was very sick. She had been that way "a long, long time." She left the camera pointed at her mother while she went away to deal with her dogs. The doctors had gathered around and studied the situation for quite some time, then issued their diagnosis.

She was dead, of course, by any definition medical science had accepted for the last century.

Someone had wired her to a robot doctor, probably during the final stages of the epidemic. It was capable of doing just about anything to keep a patient alive and was not programmed to understand brain death. That was a decision left to the human doctor, when he or she arrived.

The doctor had never arrived. The doctor was dead, and the thing that had been Charlie's mother lived on. Bach wondered if the verb "to live" had ever been so abused.

All of its arms and legs were gone, victims of gangrene. Not much else could be seen of it, but a forest of tubes and wires entered and emerged. Fluids seeped slowly through the tissue. Machines had taken over the function of every vital organ.

There were patches of greenish skin here and there, including one on the side of its head which Charlie had kissed before leaving. Bach hastily took another drink as she recalled that, and signaled the waiter for another.

Blume and Wilhelm had been fascinated. They were dubious that any part of it could still be alive, even in the sense of cell cultures. There was no way to find out, because the Charlie Station computer—Tik-Tok, to the little girl—refused access to the autodoctor's data outputs.

But there was a very interesting question that emerged as soon as everyone was convinced Charlie's mother *had* died thirty years ago.

"Hello, Anna-Louise. Sorry I'm late."

She looked up and saw Megan Galloway approaching.

Bach had not met the woman in just over ten years, though she, like almost everyone else, had seen her frequently on the tube.

Galloway was tall, for an Earth woman, and not as thin as Bach remembered her. But that was understandable, considering the recent change in her life. Her hair was fiery red and curly, which it had not been ten years ago. It might even be her natural color; she was almost nude, and the colors matched, though that didn't have to mean much. But it looked right on her.

She wore odd-looking silver slippers, and her upper body was traced by a quite lovely filigree of gilded, curving lines. It was some sort of tattoo, and it was all that was left of the machine called the Golden Gypsy. It was completely symbolic. Being the Golden Gypsy was worth a lot of money to Galloway.

Megan Galloway had broken her neck while still in her teens. She became part of the early development of a powered exoskeleton, research that led to the hideously expensive and beautiful Golden Gypsy, of which only one was ever built. It abolished wheelchairs and crutches for her. It returned her to life, in her own mind, and it made her a celebrity.

An odd by-product to learning to use an exoskeleston was the development of skills that made it possible to excel in the new technology of emotional recording: the "feelies." The world was briefly treated to the sight of quadriplegics dominating a new art form. It made Galloway famous as the best of the Trans-sisters. It made her rich, as her trans-tapes out-sold everyone else's. She made herself extremely rich by investing wisely, then she and a friend of Bach's had made her fabulously rich by being the first to capture the experience of falling in love on a trans-tape.

In a sense, Galloway had cured herself. She had always donated a lot of money to neurological research, never really expecting it to pay off. But it did, and three years ago she had thrown the Golden Gypsy away forever.

Bach had thought her cure was complete, but now she wondered. Galloway carried a beautiful crystal cane. It didn't seem to be for show. She leaned on it heavily, and made her way through the tables slowly. Bach started to get up.

"No, no, don't bother," Galloway said. "It takes me a while but I get there." She flashed that famous smile with the gap between her front teeth. There was something about the woman; the smile was so powerful that Bach found herself smiling back. "It's so good to walk I don't mind taking my time."

She let the waiter pull the chair back for her, and sat down with a sigh of relief.

"I'll have a Devil's Nitelite," she told him. "And get another of whatever that was for her."

"A banana Daquiri," Bach said, surprised to find her own drink was almost gone, and a little curious to find out what a Devil's Nitelite was.

Galloway stretched as she looked up at the balloons and gliders.

"It's great to get back to the moon," she said. She made a small gesture that indicated her body. "Great to get out of my clothes. I always feel so free in here. Funny thing, though. I just *can't* get used to not wearing shoes." She lifted one foot to display a slipper. "I feel too vulnerable without them. Like I'm going to get stepped on."

"You can take your clothes off on Earth, too," Bach pointed out.

"Some places, sure. But aside from the beach, there's no place where it's *fashionable*, don't you see?"

Bach didn't, but decided not to make a thing out of it. She knew social nudity had evolved in Luna because it never got hot or cold, and that Earth would never embrace it as fully as Lunarians had.

The drinks arrived. Bach sipped hers, and eyed Galloway's, which produced a luminous smoke ring every ten seconds. Galloway chattered on about nothing in particular for a while.

"Why did you agree to see me?" Galloway asked, at last.

"Shouldn't that be my question?"

Galloway raised an eyebrow, and Bach went on.

"You've got a hell of a story. I can't figure out why you didn't just run with it. Why arrange a meeting with someone you barely knew ten years ago, and haven't seen since, and never liked even back then?"

"I always liked you, Anna-Louise," Galloway

said. She looked up at the sky. For a while she watched a couple pedaling a skycycle, then she looked at Bach again. "I feel like I owe you something. Anyway, when I saw your name I thought I should check with you. I don't want to cause you any trouble." Suddenly she looked angry. "I don't *need* the story, Bach. I don't need *any* story, I'm too big for that. I can let it go or I can use it, it makes no difference."

"Oh, that's cute," Bach said. "Maybe I don't understand how you pay your debts. Maybe they do it different on Earth."

She thought Galloway was going to get up and leave. She had reached for her cane, then thought better of it.

"I gather it doesn't matter, then, if I go with the story."

Bach shrugged. She hadn't come here to talk about Charlie, anyway.

"How is Q.M., by the way?" she said.

Galloway didn't look away this time. She sat in silence for almost a minute, searching Bach's eyes.

"I thought I was ready for that question," she said at last. "He's living in New Zealand, on a commune. From what my agents tell me, he's happy. They don't watch television, they don't marry. They worship and they screw a lot."

"Did you really give him half the profits on that . . . that tape?"

"Did give him, am giving him, and will continue to give him until the day I die. And it's half the *gross*, my dear, which is another thing entirely. He gets half of every Mark that comes in. He's made more money off it than I have . . . and he's never touched a tenthMark. It's piling up in a Swiss account I started in his name."

"Well, he never sold anything."

Bach hadn't meant that to be as harsh as it came out, but Galloway did not seem bothered by it. The thing she had sold ...

Had there ever been anyone as thoroughly betrayed as Q.M. Cooper? Bach wondered. She might have loved him herself, but he fell totally in love with Megan Galloway.

And Galloway fell in love with him. There could be no mistake about that. Doubters are referred to *Gitana de Oro* catalog #1, an emotional recording entitled, simply, "Love." Put it in your trans-tape player, don the headset, punch PLAY, and you will experience just how hard and how completely Galloway fell in love with Q.M. Cooper. But have your head examined first. GDO #1 had been known to precipitate suicide.

Cooper had found this an impediment to the course of true love. He had always thought that love was something between two people, something exclusive, something private. He was unprepared to have Galloway mass-produce it, put it in a box with liner notes and a price tag of LM14.95, and hawk copies in every trans-tape shop from Peoria to Tibet.

The supreme irony of it to the man, who eventually found refuge in a minor cult in a far corner of the Earth, was that the tape itself, the means of his betrayal, his humiliation, was proof that Galloway had returned his love.

And Galloway had sold it. Never mind that she had her reasons, or that they were reasons with which Bach could find considerable sympathy.

She had sold it.

All Bach ever got out of the episode was a compulsion to seek lovers who looked like the Earth-muscled Cooper. Now it seemed she might get something else. It was time to change the subject.

"What do you know about Charlie?" she asked.

"You want it all, or just a general idea?" Galloway didn't wait for an answer. "I know her real name is Charlotte Isolde Hill Perkins-Smith. I know her father is dead, and her mother's condition is open to debate. Leda Perkins-Smith has a lot of money—if she's alive. Her daughter would inherit, if she's dead. I know the names of ten of Charlie's dogs. And, oh yes, I know that, appearances to the contrary, she is thirty-seven years old."

"Your source is very up-to-date."

"It's a very good source."

"You want to name him?"

"I'll pass on that, for the moment." She regarded Bach easily, her hands folded on the table in front of her. "So. What do you want me to do?"

"Is it really that simple?"

"My producers will want to kill me, but I'll sit on the story for at least twenty-four hours if you tell me to. By the way," she turned in her seat and crooked a finger at another table. "It's probably time you met my producers."

Bach turned slightly, and saw them coming toward her table.

"These are the Myers twins, Joy and Jay. Waiter, do you know how to make a Shirley Temple and a Roy Rogers?"

The waiter said he did, and went off with the order while Joy and Jay pulled up chairs and sat in them, several feet from the table but very close to each other. They had not offered to shake hands. Both were armless, with no sign of amputation, just bare, rounded shoulders. Both wore prosthetics made of golden, welded wire and powered by tiny motors. The units were one piece, fitting over their backs in a harnesslike arrangement. They were quite pretty—light and airy, perfectly articulated, cunningly wrought— and also creepy.

"You've heard of amparole?" Galloway asked. Bach shook her head. "That's the slang word for it. It's a neo-Moslem practice. Joy and Jay were convicted of murder."

"I have heard of it." She hadn't paid much attention to it, dismissing it as just another hare-brained Earthling idiocy.

"Their arms are being kept in cryonic suspension for twenty years. The theory is, if they sin no more, they'll get them back. Those prosthetics won't pick up a gun, or a knife. They won't throw a punch."

Joy and Jay were listening to this with complete stolidity. Once Bach got beyond the arms, she saw another unusual thing about them. They were dressed identically, in loose bell-bottomed trousers. Joy had small breasts, and Jay had a small mustache. Other than that, they were absolutely identical in face and body. Bach didn't care for the effect.

"They also took slices out of the cerebrums and they're on a maintenance dosage of some drug. Calms them down. You don't want to know who they killed, or how. But they were proper villains, these two."

No, I don't think I do, Bach decided. Like many cops, she looked at eyes. Joy and Jay's were calm, placid ... and deep inside was a steel-gray coldness.

"If they try to get naughty again, the amparole units go on strike. I suppose they might find a way to kill with their feet."

The twins glanced at each other, held each other's gaze for a moment, and exchanged wistful smiles. At least, Bach hoped they were just wistful.

"Yeah, okay," Bach said.

"Don't worry about them. They can't be offended with the drugs they're taking."

"I wasn't worried," Bach said. She couldn't have cared less what the freaks felt; she wished they'd been executed.

"Are they really twins?" she finally asked, against her better judgment.

"Really. One of them had a sex change, I don't know which one. And to answer your next question, yes they do, but only in the privacy of their own room."

"I wasn't—"

"And your other question . . . they are *very* good at what they do. Who am I to judge about the other? And I'm in a highly visible industry. It never hurts to have conversation pieces around. You need to get noticed."

Bach was staring to get angry, and she was not quite sure why. Maybe it was the way Galloway so cheerfully admitted her base motives, even when no one had accused her of having them.

"We were talking about the story," she said.

"We need to go with it," Joy said, startling Bach. Somehow, she had not really expected the cyborg-thing to talk. "Our source is good and the security in the story is tight—"

"—but it's dead certain to come out in twenty-four hours," Jay finished for her.

"Maybe less," Joy added.

"Shut up," Galloway said, without heat. "Anna-Louise, you were about to tell me your feeling on the matter."

Bach finished her drink as the waiter arrived with more. She caught herself staring as the twins took theirs. The metal hands were marvels of complexity. They moved just as cleverly as real hands.

"I was considering leaking the story myself. It looked like things were going against Charlie. I thought they might just let the station crash and then swear us all to secrecy."

"It strikes me," Galloway said, slowly, "that today's developments give her an edge."

"Yeah. But I don't envy her."

"Me, either. But it's not going to be easy to neglect a girl whose body may hold the secret of eternal life. If you do, somebody's bound to ask awkward questions later."

"It may not be eternal life," Bach said.

"What do you call it, then?" Jay asked.

"Why do you say that?" Joy wanted to know.

"All we know is she's lived thirty years without growing any older—externally. They'd have to examine her a lot closer to find out what's actually happening."

"And there's pressure to do so."

"Exactly. It might be the biggest medical break-through in a thousand years. What I think has happened to her is not eternal life, but extended youth."

Galloway looked thoughtful. "You know, of the two, I think extended youth would be more popular."

"I think you're right."

They brooded over that in silence for a while. Bach signaled the waiter for another drink.

"Anyway," she went on, "Charlie doesn't seem to need protection just now. But she may, and quickly."

"So you aren't in favor of letting her die."

Bach looked up, surprised and beginning to be offended, then she remembered Doctor Wilhelm. The good Doctor was not a monster, and Galloway's question was a reasonable one, given the nature of Neuro-X.

"There has to be a way to save her, *and* protect ourselves from her. That's what I'm working toward, anyway."

"Let me get this straight, then. You were thinking of leaking the story so the public outcry would force the police to save her?"

"Sure I thought . . ." Bach trailed off, suddenly realizing what Galloway was saying. "You mean you think—"

Galloway waved her hand impatiently.

"It depends on a lot of things, but mostly on how the story is handled. If you start off with the plague story, there could be pressure to blast her out of the skies and have done with it." She looked at Jay and Joy, who went into a trance-like state.

"Sure, sure," Jay said. "The plague got big play. Almost everybody remembers it. Use horror show tapes of the casualties . . ."

". . . line up the big brains to start the scare," Joy said.

"You can even add sob stuff, after it gets rolling."

"What a tragedy, this little girl has to die for the good of us all."

"Somber commentary, the world watches as she cashes in."

"You could make it play. No problem."

Bach's head had been ping-ponging between the two of them. When Galloway spoke, it was hard to swing around and look at her.

"Or you could start off with the little girl," Galloway prompted.

"*Much* better," Joy said. "Twice the story there. Indignant exposé stuff: 'Did you know, fellow citizens . . .'"

" ' . . . there's this little girl, this innocent child, swinging around up there in space and she's going to *die!* ' "

"A *rich* little girl, too, and her dying mother."

"Later, get the immortality angle."

"Not too soon," Joy cautioned. "At first, she's ordinary. Second lead is, she's got money."

"Third lead, she holds the key to eternal youth."

"Immortality."

"Youth, honey, youth. Who the fuck knows what living forever is like? Youth you can sell. It's the *only* thing you can sell."

"Megan, this it the biggest story since Jesus."

"Or at least we'll *make* it the biggest story."

"See why they're so valuable?" Galloway said. Bach hardly heard her. She was re-assessing what she had thought she knew about the situation.

"I don't know what to do," she finally confessed. "I don't know what to ask you to do, either. I guess you ought to go with what you think is best."

Galloway frowned.

"Both for professional and personal reasons, I'd rather try to help her. I'm not sure why. She is dangerous, you know."

"I realize that. But I can't believe she can't be handled."

"Neither can I." She glanced at her watch. "Tell you what, you come with us on a little trip."

Bach protested at first, but Galloway would not be denied, and Bach's resistance was at a low ebb.

By speedboat, trolley, and airplane they quickly made their way to the top of Mozartplatz, where Bach found herself in a four-seat PTP—or point-to-point—ballistic vehicle.

She had never ridden in a PTP. They were rare, mostly because they wasted a lot of energy for only a few minutes' gain in travel time. Most people took the tubes, which reached speeds of three thousand miles per hour, hovering inches above their induction rails in Luna's excellent vacuum.

But for a celebrity like Galloway, the PTP made sense. She had trouble going places in public without getting mobbed. And she certainly had the money to spare.

There was a heavy initial acceleration, then weightlessness. Bach had never liked it, and enjoyed it even less with a few drinks in her.

Little was said during the short journey. Bach had not asked where they were going, and Galloway did not volunteer it. Bach looked out one of the wide windows at the fleeting moonscape.

As she counted the valleys, rilles, and craters flowing past beneath her, she soon realized her destination. It was a distant valley, in the sense that no tube track ran through it. In a little over an hour, Tango Charlie would come speeding through, no more than a hundred meters from the surface.

The PTP landed itself in a cluster of transparent, temporary domes. There were over a hundred of them, and more PTP's than Bach had ever seen before. She decided most of the people in and around the domes fell into three categories. There were the very wealthy, owners of private spacecraft, who had erected most of these portable Xanadus and filled them with their friends. There were civic dignitaries in city-owned domes. And there were the news media.

This last category was there in its teeming hundreds. It was not what they would call a *big*

story, but it was a very visual one. It should yield
spectacular pictures for the evening news.

A long, wide black stripe had been created
across the sundrenched plain, indicating the path
Tango Charlie would take. Many cameras and
quite a few knots of pressure-suited spectators
were situated smack in the middle of that line,
with many more off to one side, to get an angle
on the approach. Beyond it were about a hundred
large glass-roofed touring buses and a motley
assortment of private crawlers, sunskimmers,
jetsleds and even some hikers: the common people, come to see the event.

Bach followed along behind the uncommon
people: Galloway, thin and somehow spectral in
the translucent suit, leaning on her crystal cane;
the Myers twins, whose amparolee arms would
not fit in the suits, so that the empty sleeves
stuck out, bloated, like crucified ghosts; and most
singular of all, the wire-sculpture arm units themselves, walking independently, on their fingertips,
looking like some demented, disjointed mechanical camel as they lurched through the dust.

They entered the largest of the domes, set on
the edge of the gathering nearest the black line,
which put it no more than a hundred meters
from the expected passage.

The first person Bach saw, as she was removing
her helmet, was Hoeffer.

He did not see her immediately. He, and many
of the other people in the dome, were watching
Galloway. So she saw his face as his gaze moved
from the celebrity to Joy and Jay ... and saw
amazement and horror, far too strong to be
simple surprise at their weirdness. It was a look
of recognition.

Galloway had said she had an excellent source.
She noticed Bach's interest, smiled, and nodded

slightly. Still struggling to remove her suit, she approached Bach.

"That's right. The twins heard a rumor something interesting might be going on at NavTrack, so they found your commander. Turns out he has rather odd sexual tastes, though it's probably fairly pedestrian to Joy and Jay. They scratched his itch, and he spilled everything."

"I find that . . . rather interesting," Bach admitted.

"I thought you would. Were you planning to make a career out of being an R/A in Navigational Tracking?"

"That wasn't my intention."

"I didn't think so. Listen, don't touch it. I can handle it without there being any chance of it backfiring on you. Within the week you'll be promoted out of there."

"I don't know if . . ."

"If what?" Galloway was looking at her narrowly.

Bach hesitated only a moment.

"I may be stiff-necked, but I'm not a fool. Thank you."

Galloway turned away a little awkwardly, then resumed struggling with her suit. Bach was about to offer some help, when Galloway frowned at her.

"How come you're not taking off your pressure suit?"

"That dome up there is pretty strong, but it's only one layer. Look around you. Most of the natives have just removed their helmets, and a lot are carrying those around. Most of the Earthlings are out of their suits. They don't understand vacuum."

"You're saying it's not safe?"

"No. But vacuum doesn't forgive. It's trying to kill you *all* the time."

Galloway looked dubious, but stopped trying to remove her suit.

Bach wandered the electronic wonderland, helmet in hand.

Tango Charlie would not be visible until less than a minute before the close encounter, and then would be hard to spot as it would be only a few seconds of arc above the horizon line. But there were cameras hundreds of miles downtrack which could already see it, both as a bright star, moving visibly against the background, and as a jittery image in some very long lenses. Bach watched as the wheel filled one screen until she could actually see furniture behind one of the windows.

For the first time since arriving, she thought of Charlie. She wondered if Tik-Tok—no, dammit, if the Charlie Station Computer had told her of the approach, and if so, would Charlie watch it. Which window would she choose? It was shocking to think that, if she chose the right one, Bach might catch a glimpse of her.

Only a few minutes to go. Knowing it was stupid, Bach looked along the line indicated by the thousand cameras, hoping to catch the first glimpse.

She saw Megan Galloway doing a walk-around, followed by a camera crew, no doubt saying bright, witty things to her huge audience. Galloway was here less for the event itself than for the many celebrities who had gathered to witness it. Bach saw her approach a famous TV star, who smiled and embraced her, making some sort of joke about Galloway's pressure suit.

You can meet him if you want, she told herself. She was a little surprised to discover she had no interest in doing so.

She saw Joy and Jay in heated conversation with Hoeffer. The twins seemed distantly amused.

She saw the countdown clock, ticking toward one minute.

Then the telescopic image in one of the remote cameras began to shake violently. In a few seconds, it had lost its fix on Charlie Station. Bach watched as annoyed technicians struggled to get it back.

"Seismic activity," one of them said, loud enough for Bach to hear.

She looked at the other remote monitor, which showed Tango Charlie as a very bright star sitting on the horizon. As she watched, the light grew visibly, until she could see it as a disc. And in another part of the screen, at a site high in the lunar hills, there was a shower of dust and rock. That must be the seismic activity, she thought. The camera operator zoomed in on this eruption, and Bach frowned. She couldn't figure out what sort of lunar quake could cause such a commotion. It looked more like an impact. The rocks and dust particles were fountaining up with lovely geometrical symmetry, each piece, from the largest boulder to the smallest mote, moving at about the same speed and in a perfect mathematical trajectory, unimpeded by any air resistance, in a way that could never be duplicated on Earth. It was a dull gray expanding dome shape, gradually flattening on top.

Frowning, she turned her attention to the spot on the plain where she had been told Charlie would first appear. She saw the first light of it, but more troubling, she saw a dozen more of the expanding domes. From here, they seemed no larger than soap bubbles.

Then another fountain of rock erupted, not far

from the impromptu parking lot full of tourist
buses.

Suddenly she knew what was happening.

"It's shooting at us!" she shouted. Everyone fell
silent, and as they were still turning to look at
her, she yelled again. "Suit up."

Her voice was drowned out by the sound every
Lunarian dreads: the high, haunting shriek of
escaping air.

Step number one, she heard a long-ago instruc-
tor say. See to *your own* pressure integrity *first*.
You can't help anybody, man, woman or child, if
you pass out before you get into your suit.

It was a five-second operation to don and seal
her helmet, one she had practiced a thousand
times as a child. She glimpsed a great hole in the
plastic roof. Debris was pouring out of it, swept
up in the sudden wind: paper, clothing, a couple
of helmets . . .

Sealed up, she looked around and realized
many of these people were doomed. They were
not in their suits, and there was little chance they
could put them on in time.

She remembered the next few seconds in a
series of vivid impressions.

A boulder, several tons of dry lunar rock,
crashed down on a bank of television monitors.

A chubby little man, his hands shaking, unable
to get his helmet over his bald head. Bach tore it
from his hands, slapped it in place, and gave it a
twist hard enough to knock him down.

Joy and Jay, as good as dead, killed by the
impossibility of fitting the mechanical arms into
their suits, holding each other calmly in metallic
embrace.

Beyond the black line, a tour bus rising slowly
in the air, turning end over end. A hundred of the

hideous gray domes of explosions growing like mushrooms all through the valley.

And there was Galloway. She was going as fast as she could, intense concentration on her face as she stumbled along after her helmet, which was rolling on the ground. Blood had leaked from one corner of her nose. It was almost soundless in the remains of the dome now.

Bach snagged the helmet, and hit Galloway with a flying tackle. Just like a drill: put helmet in place, twist, hit three snap-interlocks, then the emergency pressurization switch. She saw Galloway howl in pain and try to put her hands to her ears.

Lying there she looked up as the last big segment of the dome material lifted in a dying wind to reveal ... Tango Charlie.

It was a little wheel rolling on the horizon. No bigger than a coin.

She blinked.

And it was *here*. Vast, towering, coming directly at her through a hell of burning dust.

It was the dust that finally made the lasers visible. The great spokes of light were flashing on and off in millisecond bursts, and in each pulse a trillion dust motes were vaporized in an eyeball-frying purple light.

It was impossible that she saw it for more than a tenth of a second, but it seemed much longer. The sight would remain with her, and not just in memory. For days afterward her vision was scored with a spiderweb of purple lines.

But much worse was the awesome grandeur of the thing, the whirling menace of it as it came rushing out of the void. That picture would last much longer than a few days. It would come out only at night, in dreams that would wake her for years, drenched in sweat.

And the last strong image she would carry away from the valley was of Galloway, turned over now, pointing her crystal cane at the wheel, already far away on the horizon. A line of red laser light came out of the end of the cane and stretched away into infinity.

"Wow!" said Charlotte Isolde Hill Perkins-Smith. "Wow, Tik-Tok, that was great! Let's do it again."

Hovering in the dead center of the hub, Charlie had watched all of the encounter. It had been a lot like she imagined a roller-coaster would be when she watched the films in Tik-Tok's memory. If it had a fault—and she wasn't complaining, far from it—it was that the experience had been too short. For almost an hour she had watched the moon get bigger, until it no longer seemed round and the landscape was rolling by beneath her. But she'd seen that much before. This time it just got larger and larger, and faster and faster, until she was scooting along at about a zillion miles an hour. Then there was a lot of flashing lights . . . and gradually, the ground got farther away again. It was still back there, dwindling, no longer very interesting.

"I'm glad you liked it," Tik-Tok said.

"Only one thing. How come I had to put on my pressure suit?"

"Just a precaution."

She shrugged, and made her way to the elevator. When she got out at the rim, she frowned. There were alarms sounding, far around the rim on the wheel.

"We got a problem?" she asked.

"Minor," Tik-Tok said.

"What happened?"

"We got hit by some rocks."

"We must of passed *real* close!"

"Charlie, if you'd been down here when we passed, you could have reached out and written your name on a rock."

She giggled at that idea, then hurried off to see to the dogs.

It was about two hours later that Anna-Louise called. Charlie was inclined to ignore it, she had so much to do, but in the end, she sat down in front of the camera. Anna-Louise was there, and sitting beside her was another woman.

"Are you okay, Charlie?" Anna wanted to know.

"Why shouldn't I be?" Damn, she thought. She wasn't supposed to answer a question with another question. But then, what right did Anna have to ask her to do that?

"I was wondering if you were watching a little while ago, when you passed so close to the moon."

"I sure was. It was great."

There was a short pause. The two women looked at each other, then Anna-Louise sighed, and faced Charlie again.

"Charlie, there are a few things I have to tell you."

As in most disasters involving depressurization, there was not a great demand for first aid. Most of the bad injuries were fatal.

Galloway was not hearing too well and Bach still had spots before her eyes; Hoeffer hadn't even bumped his head.

The body-count was not complete, but it was going to be high.

For a perilous hour after the passage, there was talk of shooting Tango Charlie out of the sky.

Much of the advisory team had already gathered in the meeting room by the time Bach and Hoeffer arrived—with Galloway following closely

behind. A hot debate was in progress. People
recognized Galloway, and a few seemed inclined
to question her presence here, but Hoeffer shut
them up quickly. A deal had been struck in the
PTP, on the way back from the disaster. The fix
was in, and Megan Galloway was getting an
exclusive on the story. Galloway had proved to
Hoeffer that Joy and Jay had kept tapes of his
security lapse.

The eventual explanation for the unprovoked
and insane attack was simple. The Charlie Station Computer had been instructed to fire upon
any object approaching within five kilometers. It
had done so, faithfully, for thirty years, not that
it ever had much to shoot at. The close approach
of Luna must have been an interesting problem.
Tik-Tok was no fool. Certainly he would know the
consequences of his actions. But a computer did
not think at all like a human, no matter how
much it might sound like one. There were rigid
hierarchies in a brain like Tik-Tok. One part of
him might realize something was foolish, but be
helpless to over-ride a priority order.

Analysis of the pattern of laser strikes helped to
confirm this. The hits were totally random. Vehi-
cles, domes, and people had not been targeted;
however, if they were in the way, they were hit.

The one exception to the randomness concerned
the black line Bach had seen. Tik-Tok had found
a way to avoid shooting directly ahead of himself
without violating his priority order. Thus, he
avoided stirring up debris that Charlie Station
would be flying through in another few seconds.

The decision was made to take no reprisals on
Tango Charlie. Nobody was happy about it, but
no one could suggest anything short of total
destruction.

But action had to be taken now. Very soon the

public was going to wonder why this dangerous object had not been destroyed before the approach. The senior police present and the representatives of the Mayor's office all agreed that the press would have to be let in. They asked Galloway if they could have her cooperation in the management of this phase.

And Bach watched as, with surprising speed, Megan Galloway took over the meeting.

"You need time right now," she said, at one point. "The best way to get it is to play the little-girl angle, and play it hard. You were not so heartless as to endanger the little girl—and you had no reason to believe the station was any kind of threat. What you have to do now is tell the truth about what we know, and what's been done."

"How about the immortality angle?" someone asked.

"What about it? It's going to leak someday. Might as well get it out in front of us."

"But it will prejudice the public in favor of . . ." Wilhelm looked around her, and decided not to finish her objection.

"It's a price we have to pay," Galloway said, smoothly. "You folks will do what you think is right. I'm sure of that. You wouldn't let public opinion influence your decision."

Nobody had anything to say to that. Bach managed not to laugh.

"The big thing is to answer the questions before they get asked. I suggest you get started on your statements, then call in the press. In the meantime, Corporal Bach has invited me to listen in on her next conversation with Charlie Perkins-Smith, so I'll leave you now."

Bach led Galloway down the corridor toward the operations room, shaking her head in admiration. She looked over her shoulder.

"I got to admit it. You're very smooth."

"It's my profession. You're pretty smooth, yourself."

"What do you mean?"

"I mean I owe you. I'm afraid I owe you more than I'll be able to repay."

Bach stopped, honestly bewildered.

"You saved my *life*," Galloway shouted. "*Thank you!*"

"So what if I did? You don't owe me anything. It's not the custom."

"What's not the custom?"

"You can be grateful, sure. I'd be, if somebody pressurized me. But it would be an insult to try to pay me back for it. Like on the desert, you know, you have to give water to somebody dying of thirst."

"Not in the deserts I've been to," Galloway said. They were alone in the hallway. Galloway seemed distressed, and Bach felt awkward. "We seem to be at a cultural impasse. I feel I owe you a lot, and you say it's nothing."

"No problem," Bach pointed out. "You were going to help me get promoted out of this stinking place. Do that, and we'll call it even."

Galloway was shaking her head.

"I don't think I'll be able to, now. You know that fat man you stuffed into a helmet, before you got to me? He asked me about you. He's the Mayor of Clavius. He'll be talking to the Mayor of New Dresden, and you'll get the promotion and a couple of medals and maybe a reward, too."

They regarded each other uneasily. Bach knew that gratitude could equal resentment. She thought she could see some of that in Galloway's eyes. But there was determination, too. Megan Galloway paid her debts. She had been paying one to Q.M. Cooper for ten years.

By unspoken agreement they left it at that, and went to talk to Charlie.

Most of the dogs didn't like the air blower. Mistress Too White O'Hock was the exception. 2-White would turn her face into the stream of warm air as Charlie directed the hose over her sable pelt, then she would let her tongue hang out in an expression of such delight that Charlie would usually end up laughing at her.

Charlie brushed the fine hair behind 2-White's legs, the hair that was white almost an inch higher than it should be on a champion Sheltie. Just one little inch, and 2-White was sterilized. She would have been a fine mother. Charlie had seen her looking at puppies whelped by other mothers, and she knew it made 2-White sad.

But you can't have everything in this world. Tik-Tok had said that often enough. And you can't let all your dogs breed, or pretty soon you'll be knee deep in dogs. Tik-Tok said that, too.

In fact, Tik-Tok said a lot of things Charlie wished were not true. But he had never lied to her.

"Were you listening?" she asked.

"During your last conversation? Of course I was."

Charlie put 2-White down on the floor, and summoned the next dog. This was Engelbert, who wasn't a year old yet, and still inclined to be frisky when he shouldn't be. Charlie had to scold him before he would be still.

"Some of the things she said," Tik-Tok began. "It seemed like she disturbed you. Like how old you are."

"That's silly," Charlie said, quickly. "I knew how old I am." This was the truth . . . and yet it wasn't everything. Her first four dogs were all dead. The oldest had been thirteen. There had been many dogs since then. Right now, the oldest

dog was sixteen, and sick. He wouldn't last much
longer.

"I just never added it up," Charlie said,
truthfully.

"There was never any reason to."

"But I don't grow up," she said, softly. "Why is
that, Tik-Tok?"

"I don't know, Charlie."

"Anna said if I go down to the moon, they
might be able to find out."

Tik-Tok didn't say anything.

"Was she telling the truth? About all those
people who got hurt?"

"Yes."

"Maybe I shouldn't have got mad at her."

Again, Tik-Tok was silent. Charlie had been
very angry. Anna and a new woman, Megan, had
told her all these awful things, and when they
were done Charlie knocked over the television
equipment and went away. That had been almost
a day ago, and they had been calling back almost
all the time.

"Why did you do it?" she said.

"I didn't have any choice."

Charlie accepted that. Tik-Tok was a mechanical man, not like her at all. He was a faithful
guardian and the closest thing she had to a
friend, but she knew he was different. For one
thing, he didn't have a body. She had sometimes
wondered if this inconvenienced him any, but she
had never asked.

"Is my mother really dead?"

"Yes."

Charlie stopped brushing. Engelbert looked
around at her, then waited patiently until she
told him he could get down.

"I guess I knew that."

"I thought you did. But you never asked."

"She was someone to talk to," Charlie explained. She left the grooming room and walked down the promenade. Several dogs followed behind her, trying to get her to play.

She went into her mother's room and stood for a moment looking at the thing in the bed. Then she moved from machine to machine, flipping switches, until everything was quiet. And when she was done, that was the only change in the room. The machines no longer hummed, rumbled, and clicked. The thing on the bed hadn't changed at all. Charlie supposed she could keep on talking to it, if she wanted to, but she suspected it wouldn't be the same.

She wondered if she ought to cry. Maybe she should ask Tik-Tok, but he'd never been very good with those kind of questions. Maybe it was because he couldn't cry himself, so he didn't know when people ought to cry. But the fact was, Charlie had felt a lot sadder at Albert's funeral.

In the end, she sang her hymn again, then closed and locked the door behind her. She would never go in there again.

"She's back," Steiner called across the room. Bach and Galloway hastily put down their cups of coffee and hurried over to Bach's office.

"She just plugged his camera in," Steiner explained, as they took their seats. "Looks a little different, doesn't she?"

Bach had to agree. They had glimpsed her in other cameras as she went about her business. Then, about an hour ago, she had entered her mother's room again. From there, she had gone to her own room, and when she emerged, she was a different girl. Her hair was washed and combed. She wore a dress that seemed to have started off as a woman's blouse. The sleeves had been cut off and bits of it had been inexpertly taken in. There was red polish on her nails. Her face was heavily made up. It was overdone, and completely wrong for someone of her apparent age, but it was not the wild, almost tribal paint she had worn before.

Charlie was seated behind a huge wooden desk, facing the camera.

"Good morning, Anna and Megan," she said, solemnly.

"Good morning, Charlie," Galloway said.

"I'm sorry I shouted at you," Charlie said. Her hands were folded carefully in front of her. There was a sheet of paper just to the left of them; other than that, the desk was bare. "I was confused and upset, and I needed some time to think about the things you said."

"That's all right," Bach told her. She did her best to conceal a yawn. She and Galloway had been awake for a day and a half. There had been a few catnaps, but they were always interrupted by sightings of Charlie.

"I've talked things over with Tik-Tok," Charlie went on. "And I turned my mother off. You were right. She was dead, anyway."

Bach could think of nothing to say to that. She glanced at Galloway, but could read nothing in the other woman's face.

"I've decided what I want to do," Charlie said. "But first I—"

"Charlie," Galloway said, quickly, "could you show me what you have there on the table?"

There was a brief silence in the room. Several people turned to look at Galloway, but nobody said anything. Bach was about to, but Galloway was making a motion with her hand, under the table, where no one but Bach was likely to see it. Bach decided to let it ride for the moment.

Charlie was looking embarrassed. She reached

for the paper, glanced at it, then looked back at the camera.

"I drew this picture for you," she said. "Because I was sorry I shouted."

"Could I see it?"

Charlie jumped down off the chair and came around to hold the picture up. She seemed proud of it, and she had every right to be. Here at last was visual proof that Charlie was not what she seemed to be. No eight-year-old could have drawn this fine pencil portrait of a Sheltie.

"This is for Anna," she said.

"That's very nice, Charlie," Galloway said. "I'd like one, too."

"I'll draw you one!" Charlie said happily . . . and ran out of the picture.

There was angry shouting for a few moments. Galloway stood her ground, explaining that she had only been trying to cement the friendship, and how was she to know Charlie would run off like that?

Even Hoeffer was emboldened enough to take a few shots, pointing out—logically, in Bach's opinion—that time was running out and if anything was to be done about her situation every second was valuable.

"All right, all right, so I made a mistake. I promise I'll be more careful next time. Anna, I hope you'll call me when she comes back." And with that, she picked up her cane and trudged from the room.

Bach was surprised. It didn't seem like Galloway to leave the story before it was over, even if nothing was happening. But she was too tired to worry about it. She leaned back in her chair, closed her eyes, and was asleep in less than a minute.

*   *   *

Charlie was hard at work on the picture for Megan when Tik-Tok interrupted her. She looked up in annoyance.

"Can't you see I'm busy?"

"I'm sorry, but this can't wait. There's a telephone call for you."

"There's a . . . *what?*"

But Tik-Tok said no more. Charlie went across the room to the phone, silent these thirty years. She eyed it suspiciously, then pressed the button. As she did, dim memories flooded through her. She saw her mother's face. For the first time, she felt like crying.

"This is Charlotte Perkins-Smith," she said, in a childish voice. "My mother isn't . . . my mother . . . may I ask who's calling, please?"

There was no picture on the screen, but after a short pause, there was a familiar voice.

"This is Megan Galloway, Charlie. Can we talk?"

When Steiner shook Bach's shoulder, she opened her eyes to see Charlie sitting on the desk once more. Taking a quick sip of the hot coffee Steiner had brought, she tried to wipe the cobwebs from her mind and get back to work. The girl was just sitting there, hands folded once more.

"Hello, Anna," the girl said. "I just wanted to call and tell you I'll do whatever you people think is best. I've been acting silly. I hope you'll forgive me; it's been a long time since I had to talk to other people."

"That's okay, Charlie."

"I'm sorry I pissed on Captain Hoeffer. Tik-Tok said that was a bad thing to do, and that I ought to be more respectful to him, since he's the guy in charge. So if you'll get him, I'll do whatever he says."

"All right, Charlie. I'll get him."

Bach got up and watched Hoeffer take her chair.

"You'll be talking just to me from now on," he said, with what he must have felt was a friendly smile. "Is that all right?"

"Sure," Charlie said, indifferently.

"You can go get some rest now, Corporal Bach," Hoeffer said. She saluted, and turned on her heel. She knew it wasn't fair to Charlie to feel betrayed, but she couldn't help it. True, she hadn't talked to the girl all that long. There was no reason to feel a friendship had developed. But she felt sick watching Hoeffer talk to her. The man would lie to her, she was sure of that.

But then, could she have done any different? It was a disturbing thought. The fact was, there had as yet been no orders on what to do about Charlie. She was all over the news, the public debate had begun, and Bach knew it would be another day before public officials had taken enough soundings to know which way they should leap. In the meantime, they had Charlie's cooperation, and that was good news.

Bach wished she could be happier about it.

"Anna, there's a phone call for you."

She took it at one of the vacant consoles. When she pushed the Talk button, a light came on indicating the other party wanted privacy, so she picked up the handset and asked who was calling.

"Anna," said Galloway, "come at once to room 569 in the Pension Kleist. That's four corridors from the main entrance to NavTrack, level—"

"I can find it. What's this all about? You got your story."

"I'll tell you when you get there."

The first person Bach saw in the small room

was Ludmilla Rossnikova, the computer expert from GMA. She was sitting in a chair across the room, looking uncomfortable. Bach shut the door behind her, and saw Galloway sprawled in another chair before a table littered with electronic gear.

"I felt I had to speak to Tik-Tok privately," Galloway began, without preamble. She looked about as tired as Bach felt.

"Is that why you sent Charlie away?"

Galloway gave her a truly feral grin, and for a moment did not look tired at all. Bach realized she loved this sort of intrigue, loved playing fast and loose, taking chances.

"That's right. I figured Ms. Rossnikova was the woman to get me through, so now she's working for me."

Bach was impressed. It would not have been cheap to hire Rossnikova away from GMA. She would not have thought it possible.

"GMA doesn't know that, and it won't know, if you can keep a secret," Galloway went on. "I assured Ludmilla that you could."

"You mean she's spying for you."

"Not at all. She's not going to be working against GMA's interests, which are quite minimal in this affair. We're just not going to tell them about her work for me, and next year Ludmilla will take early retirement and move into a dacha in Georgia she's coveted all her life."

Bach looked at Rossnikova, who seemed embarrassed. So everybody has her price, Bach thought. So what else is new?

"Turns out she had a special code which she withheld from the folks back at NavTrack. I suspected she might. I wanted to talk to him without anyone else knowing I was doing it. Your control room was a bit crowded for that. Ludmilla, you want to take it from there?"

She did, telling Bach the story in a low voice, with reserved, diffident gestures. Bach wondered if she would be able to live with her defection, decided she'd probably get over it soon enough.

Rossnikova had raised Charlie Station, which in this sense was synonymous with Tik-Tok, the station computer. Galloway had talked to him. She wanted to know what he knew. As she suspected, he was well aware of his own orbital dynamics. He knew he was going to crash into the moon. So what did he intend to do about Charlotte Perkins-Smith? Galloway wanted to know.

What are you offering? Tik-Tok responded.

"The important point is, he doesn't want Charlie to die. He can't do anything about his instruction to fire on intruders. But he claims he would have let Charlie go years ago but for one thing."

"Our quarantine probes," Bach said.

"Exactly. He's got a lifeboat in readiness. A few minutes from impact, if nothing had been resolved, he'll load Charlie in it and blast her away, after first killing both your probes. He knows it's not much of a chance, but impact on the lunar surface is no chance at all."

Bach finally sat down. She thought it over for a minute, then spread her hands.

"Great," she said. "It sounds like all our problems are solved. We'll just take this to Hoeffer, and we can call off the probes."

Galloway and Rossnikova were silent. At last, Galloway sighed.

"It may not be as simple as that."

Bach stood again, suddenly sure of what was coming next.

"I've got good sources, both in the news media

and in city hall. Things are not looking good for Charlie."

"I can't *believe* it!" Bach shouted. "They're ready to let a little girl die? They're not even going to try to save her?"

Galloway made soothing motions, and Bach gradually calmed down.

"It's not definite yet. But the trend is there. For one thing, she is *not* a little girl, as you well know. I was counting on the public perception of her as a little girl, but that's not working out so well."

"But all your stories have been so positive."

"I'm not the only newscaster. And ... the public doesn't always determine it anyway. Right now, they're in favor of Charlie, seventy-thirty. But that's declining, and a lot of that seventy percent is soft, as they say. Not sure. The talk is, the decision makers are going to make it look like an unfortunate accident. Tik-Tok will be a great help there; it'll be easy to provoke an incident that could kill Charlie."

"It's just not right," Bach said, gloomily. Galloway leaned forward and looked at her intently.

"That's what I wanted to know. Are you still on Charlie's side, all the way? And if you are, what are you willing to risk to save her?"

Bach met Galloway's intent stare. Slowly, Galloway smiled again.

"That's what I thought. Here's what I want to do."

Charlie was sitting obediently by the telephone in her room at the appointed time, and it rang just when Megan had said it would. She answered it as she had before.

"Hi there, kid. How's it going?"

"I'm fine. Is Anna there too?"

"She sure is. Want to say hi to her?"

"I wish you'd tell her it was you that told me to—"

"I already did, and she understands. Did you have any trouble?"

Charlie snorted.

"With *him?* What a doo-doo-head. He'll believe anything I tell him. Are you sure he can't hear us in here?"

"Positive. Nobody can hear us. Did Tik-Tok tell you what all you have to do?"

"I think so. I wrote some of it down."

"We'll go over it again, point by point. We can't have any mistakes."

When they got the final word on the decision, it was only twelve hours to impact. None of them had gotten any sleep since the close approach. It seemed like years ago to Bach.

"The decision is to have an accident," Galloway said, hanging up the phone. She turned to Rossnikova who bent, hollow-eyed, over her array of computer keyboards. "How's it coming with the probe?"

"I'm pretty sure I've got it now," she said, leaning back. "I'll take it through the sequence one more time." She sighed, then looked at both of them. "Every time I try to re-program it, it wants to tell me about this broken rose blossom and the corpse of a puppy and the way the wheel looks with all the lighted windows." She yawned hugely. "Some of it's kind of pretty, actually."

Bach wasn't sure what Rossnikova was talking about, but the important thing was the probe was taken care of. She looked at Galloway.

"My part is all done," Galloway said. "In record time, too."

"I'm not even going to guess what it cost you," Bach said.

"It's only money."

"What about Doctor Blume?"

"He's with us. He wasn't even very expensive. I think he wanted to do it, anyway." She looked from Bach to Rossnikova, and back again. "What do you say? Are we ready to go? Say in one hour?"

Neither of them raised an objection. Silently, they shook each other's hands. They knew it would not go easy with them if they were discovered, but that had already been discussed and accepted and there seemed no point in mentioning it again.

Bach left them in a hurry.

The dogs were more excited than Charlie had ever seen them. They sensed something was about to happen.

"They're probably just picking it up from you," Tik-Tok ventured.

"That could be it," Charlie agreed. They were leaping and running all up and down the corridor. It had been *hell* getting them all down here, by a route Tik-Tok had selected that would avoid all the operational cameras used by Captain Hoeffer and those other busybodies. But here they finally were, and there was the door to the lifeboat, and suddenly she realized that Tik-Tok could not come along.

"What are you going to do?" she finally asked him.

"That's a silly question, Charlie."

"But you'll *die!*"

"Not possible. Since I was never alive, I can't die."

"Oh, you're just playing with words." She stopped, and couldn't think of anything good to say. Why didn't they have more words? There ought to be more words, so some of them would be useful for saying goodbye.

"Did you scrubba-scrub?" Tik-Tok asked. "You want to look nice."

Charlie nodded, wiping away a tear. Things were just happening so *fast*.

"Good. Now you remember to do all the things I taught you to do. It may be a long time before you can be with people, but I think you will, someday. And in the meantime, Anna-Louise and Megan have promised me that they'll be very strict with little girls who won't pick up their rooms and wash their hair."

"I'll be good," Charlie promised.

"I want you to obey them just like you've obeyed me."

"I will."

"Good. You've been a very good little girl, and I'll expect you to continue to be a good girl. Now get in that lifeboat, and get going."

So she did, along with dozens of barking Shelties.

There was a guard outside the conference room and Bach's badge would not get her past him, so she assumed that was where the crime was being planned.

She would have to be very careful.

She entered the control room. It was understaffed, and no one was at her old chair. A few people noticed her as she sat down, but no one seemed to think anything of it. She settled down, keeping an eye on the clock.

Forty minutes after her arrival, all hell broke loose.

It had been an exciting day for the probe. New instructions had come. Any break in the routine was welcome, but this one was double good, because the new programmer wanted to know *everything*, and the probe finally got a chance to transmit its poetry. It was a hell of a load off one's mind.

When it finally managed to assure the programmer that it understood and would obey, it settled back in a cybernetic equivalent of wild expectation.

The explosion was everything it could have hoped for. The wheel tore itself apart in a ghastly silence and began spreading itself wildly to the blackness. The probe moved in, listening, listening . . .

And there it was. The soothing song it had been told to listen for, coming from a big oblong hunk of the station that moved faster than the rest of it. The probe moved in close, though it had not been told to. As the oblong flashed by the probe had time to catalog it (LIFEBOAT, type 4A; functioning) and to get just a peek into one of the portholes.

The face of a dog peered back, ears perked alertly.

The probe filed the image away for later contemplation, and then moved in on the rest of the wreckage, lasers blazing in the darkness.

Bach had a bad moment when she saw the probe move in on the lifeboat, then settled back and tried to make herself inconspicuous as the vehicle bearing Charlie and the dogs accelerated away from the cloud of wreckage.

She had been evicted from her chair, but she had expected that. As people ran around, shouting at each other, she called room 569 at the Kleist, then patched Rossnikova into her tracking computers. She was sitting at an operator's console in a corner of the room, far from the excitement.

Rossnikova was a genius. The blip vanished from her screen. If everything was going according to plan, no data about the lifeboat was going into the memory of the tracking computer.

It would be like it never existed.

Everything went so smoothly, Bach thought later. You couldn't help taking it as a good omen, even if, like Bach, you weren't superstitious. She knew nothing was going to be easy in the long run, that there were bound to be problems they hadn't thought of . . .

But all in all, you just had to be optimistic.

The remotely piloted PTP made rendezvous right on schedule. The transfer of Charlie and the dogs went like clockwork. The empty lifeboat was topped off with fuel and sent on a solar escape orbit, airless and lifeless, its only cargo a barrel of radioactive death that should sterilize it if anything would.

The PTP landed smoothly at the remote habitat Galloway's agents had located and purchased. It had once been a biological research station, so it was physically isolated in every way from lunar society. Some money changed hands, and all records of the habitat were erased from computer files.

All food, air, and water had to be brought in by crawler, over a rugged mountain pass. The habitat itself was large enough to accommodate a hundred people in comfort. There was plenty of room for the dogs. A single dish antenna was the only link to the outside world.

Galloway was well satisfied with the place. She promised Charlie that one of these days she would be paying a visit. Neither of them mentioned the reason that no one would be coming out immediately. Charlie settled in for a long stay, privately wondering if she would *ever* get any company.

One thing they hadn't planned on was alcohol. Charlie was hooked bad, and not long after her arrival she began letting people know about it.

Blume reluctantly allowed a case of whiskey to be brought in on the next crawler, reasoning that a girl in full-blown withdrawal would be impossible to handle remotely. He began a program to taper her off, but in the meantime Charlie went on a three-day bender that left her bleary-eyed.

The first biological samples sent in all died within a week. These were a guinea pig, a rhesus monkey and a chicken. The symptoms were consistent with Neuro-X, so there was little doubt the disease was still alive. A dog, sent in later, lasted eight days.

Blume gathered valuable information from all these deaths, but they upset Charlie badly. Bach managed to talk him out of further live animal experiments for at least a few months.

She had taken accumulated vacation time, and was living in a condominium on a high level of the Mozartplatz, bought by Galloway and donated to what they were coming to think of as the Charlie Project. With Galloway back on Earth and Rossnikova neither needed nor inclined to participate further, Charlie Project was Bach and Doctor Blume. Security was essential. Four people knowing about Charlie was already three too many, Galloway said.

Charlie seemed cheerful, and cooperated with Blume's requests. He worked through robotic instruments, and it was frustrating. But she learned to take her own blood and tissue samples and prepare them for viewing. Blume was beginning to learn something of the nature of Neuro-X, though he admitted that, working alone, it might take him years to reach a breakthrough. Charlie didn't seem to mind.

The isolation techniques were rigorous. The crawler brought supplies to within one hundred yards of the habitat and left them sitting there on the dust. A second crawler would come out to bring them in. Under no circumstances was anything allowed to leave the habitat, nor to come in contact with anything that was going back to the world—and, indeed, the crawler was the only thing in the latter category.

Contact was strictly one-way. Anything could go in, but nothing could come out. That was the strength of the system and its final weakness.

Charlie had been living in the habitat for fifteen days when she started running a fever. Doctor Blume prescribed bed rest and aspirin, and didn't tell Bach how worried he was.

The next day was worse. She coughed a lot, couldn't keep food down. Blume was determined to go out there in an isolation suit. Bach had to physically restrain him at one point, and be very firm with him until he finally calmed down and saw how foolish he was being. It would do Charlie no good for Blume to die.

Bach called Galloway, who arrived by express liner the next day.

By then Blume had some idea what was happening.

"I gave her a series of vaccinations," he said, mournfully. "It's so standard . . . I hardly gave it a thought. Measles-D1, the Manila-strain mumps, all the normal communicable diseases we have to be so careful of in a Lunar environment. Some of them were killed viruses, some were weakened . . . and they seem to be attacking her."

Galloway raged at him for a while. He was too depressed to fight back. Bach just listened, withholding her own judgment.

The next day he learned more. Charlie was getting things he had not inoculated her against, things that could have come in as hitch-hikers on the supplies, or that might have been lying dormant in the habitat itself.

He had carefully checked her thirty-year-old medical record. There had been no hint of any immune system deficiency, and it was not the kind of syndrome that could be missed. But somehow she had acquired it.

He had a theory. He had several of them. None would save his patient.

"Maybe the Neuro-X destroyed her immune system. But you'd think she would have succumbed to stray viruses there on the station. Unless the Neuro-X attacked the viruses, too, and changed them."

He mumbled things like that for hours on end as he watched Charlie waste away on his television screen.

"For whatever reason . . . she was in a state of equilibrium there on the station. Bringing her here destroyed that. If I could understand how, I still might save her . . ."

The screen showed a sweating, gaunt-faced little girl. Much of her hair had fallen out. She complained that her throat was very dry and she had trouble swallowing. She just keeps fighting, Bach thought, and felt the tightness in the back of her own throat.

Charlie's voice was still clear.

"Tell Megan I finally finished her picture," she said.

"She's right here, honey," Bach said. "You can tell her yourself."

"Oh." Charlie licked her lips with a dry tongue, and her eyes wandered around. "I can't see much. Are you there, Megan?"

"I'm here."

"Thanks for trying." She closed her eyes, and for a moment Bach thought she was gone. Then the eyes opened again.

"Anna-Louise?"

"I'm still right here, darling."

"Anna, what's going to happen to my dogs?"

"I'll take care of them," she lied. "Don't you worry." Somehow she managed to keep her voice steady. It was the hardest thing she had ever done.

"Good. Tik-Tok will tell you which ones to breed. They're good dogs, but you can't let them take advantage of you."

"I won't."

Charlie coughed, and seemed to become a little smaller when she was through. She tried to lift her head, could not, and coughed again. Then she smiled, just a little bit, but enough to break Bach's heart.

"I'll go see Albert," she said. "Don't go away."

"We're right here."

She closed her eyes. She continued breathing raggedly for over an hour, but her eyes never opened again.

Bach let Galloway handle the details of cleaning up and covering up. She felt listless, uninvolved. She kept seeing Charlie as she had first seen her, a painted savage in a brown tide of dogs.

When Galloway went away, Bach stayed on at the Mozartplatz, figuring the woman would tell her if she had to get out. She went back to work, got the promotion Galloway had predicted, and began to take an interest in her new job. She evicted Ralph and his barbells from her old apartment, though she continued to pay the rent on it. She grew to like Mozartplatz even more than she had expected she would, and dreaded the day Galloway would eventually sell the place. There was a broad balcony with potted plants where she could sit with her feet propped up and look out over the whole insane buzz and clatter of the place, or prop her elbows on the rail and spit into the lake, over a mile below. The weather was going to take some getting used to, though, if she ever managed to afford a place of her own here. The management sent rainfall and windstorm schedules in the mail and she faithfully posted them in the kitchen, then always forgot and got drenched.

The weeks turned into months. At the end of the sixth month, when Charlie was no longer haunting Bach's dreams, Galloway showed up. For many reasons Bach was not delighted to see her, but she put on a brave face and invited her in. She was dressed this time, Earth fashion, and she seemed a lot stronger.

"Can't stay long," she said, sitting on the couch Bach had secretly begun to think of her own. She took a document out of her pocket and put it on a table near Bach's chair. "This is the deed to this condo. I've signed it over to you, but I haven't registered it yet. There are different ways to go about it, for tax purposes, so I thought I'd check with you. I told you I always pay my debts. I was hoping to do it with Charlie, but that turned out ... well, it was more something I was doing for myself, so it didn't count."

Bach was glad she had said that. She had been wondering if she would be forced to hit her.

"This won't pay what I owe you, but it's a start." She looked at Bach and raised one eyebrow. "It's a start, whether or not you accept it. I'm hoping you won't be too stiff-necked, but with loonies—or should I say Citizens of Luna? —I've found you can never be too sure."

Bach hesitated, but only for a split second.

"Loonies, Lunarians . . . who cares?" She picked up the deed. "I accept."

Galloway nodded, and took an envelope out of the same pocket the deed had been in. She leaned back, and seemed to search for words.

"I . . . thought I ought to tell you what I've done." She waited, and Bach nodded. They both knew, without mentioning Charlie's name, what she was talking about.

"The dogs were painlessly put to sleep. The habitat was depressurized and irradiated for about a month, then reactivated. I had some animals sent in and they survived. So I sent in a robot on a crawler and had it bring these out. Don't worry, they've been checked out a thousand ways and they're absolutely clean."

She removed a few sheets of paper from the envelope and spread them out on the table. Bach leaned over and looked at the pencil sketches.

"You remember she said she'd finally finished that picture for me? I've already taken that one out. But there were these others, one with your name on it, and I wondered if you wanted any of them?"

Bach had already spotted the one she wanted. It was a self-portrait, just the head and shoulders. In it Charlie had a faint smile . . . or did she? It was that kind of drawing; the more she looked at it, the harder it was to tell just what Charlie had been thinking when she drew this. At the bottom it said, "To Anna-Louise, my friend."

Bach took it and thanked Galloway, who seemed almost as anxious to leave as Bach was to have her go.

Bach fixed herself a drink and sat back in "her" chair in "her" home. That was going to take some getting used to, but she looked forward to it.

She picked up the drawing and studied it, sipping her drink. Frowning, she stood and went through the sliding glass doors onto her balcony. There, in the brighter light of the atrium, she held the drawing up and looked closer.

There was somebody behind Charlie. But maybe that wasn't right, either, maybe it was just that she had started to draw one thing, had erased it and started again. Whatever it was, there was another network of lines in the paper that were very close to the picture that was there, but slightly different.

The longer Bach stared at it, the more she was convinced she was seeing the older woman Charlie had never had a chance to become. She seemed to be in her late thirties, not a whole lot older than Bach.

Bach took a mouthful of liquor and was about to go back inside when a wind came up and snatched the paper from her hand.

"Goddamn weather!" she shouted as she made a grab for it. But it was already twenty feet away, turning over and over and falling. She watched it dwindle past all hope of recovery.

Was she relieved?

"Can I get that for you?"

She looked up, startled, and saw a man in a flight harness, flapping like crazy to remain stationary. Those contraptions required an amazing amount of energy, and this fellow showed it, with bulging biceps and huge thigh muscles and a chest big as a barrel. The metal wings glittered and the leather strap creaked and the sweat poured off him.

"No thanks," she said, then she smiled at him. "But I'd be proud to make you a drink."

He smiled back, asked her apartment number, and flapped off toward the nearest landing platform. Bach looked down, but the paper with Charlie's face on it was already gone, vanished in the vast spaces of Mozartplatz.

Bach finished her drink, then went to answer the knock on her door.

"HEY, BROTHER!"

The kid who was golden hooked his thumbs in his belt, as Sandy and I watched the dialogue from the rigging on the side of the hull. "I'm getting tired of hanging around this Star-pit. Where you running to?"

The man who was golden clicked his nails again. "Go away, distant cousin."

"Come on, brother, give me a berth on your lifeboat."

"Go away or I'll kill you."

"Now, brother, I'm just a youngster adrift in this forsaken corner of the sky. Come on, now—"

Suddenly the blond man whirled from the railing, grabbed up a four-foot length of pipe leaning beside him, and swung it so hard it hissed. The black-haired ragamuffin leapt back and from under his rag snatched something black that, with a flick of that long nail, grew seven inches of blade. The two bodies locked, turned, fell. A gurgle, and the man's hands slipped from the neck of the ragamuffin. The boy scrambled back to his feet. Blood bubbled and popped on the hot blade.

A last spasm caught the man; he flipped over, smearing the catwalk, rolled once more, this time under the rail, and dropped—two hundred fifty feet to the cement flooring.

"Hey!" Sandy called, when he got his voice back up into his throat, "what about . . . I mean you . . . well, your ship!" There are no familial inheritance laws among golden—only rights of plunder.

The golden glanced back. "I give it to you," he sneered.

THE TOR DOUBLE NOVELS

*forthcoming

SAMUEL R. DELANY

THE STAR PIT

A TOM DOHERTY ASSOCIATES BOOK
NEW YORK

THE STAR PIT

Copyright © 1966 by Galaxy Publishing Corp.

Reprinted by permission of the author and his agent, Henry Morrison, Inc.

A TOR Book
Published by Tom Doherty Associates, Inc.
49 West 24 Street
New York, N.Y. 10010

Cover art by Tony Roberts

ISBN: 0-812-55956-8   Can. ISBN: 0-812-55957-6

First Tor edition: January 1989

Printed in the United States of America

0 9 8 7 6 5 4 3 2 1

Two glass panes with dirt between and little tunnels from cell to cell: when I was a kid I had an ant colony.

But once some of our four-to-six-year-olds built an ecologarium with six-foot plastic panels and grooved aluminum bars to hold corners and top down. They put it out on the sand.

There was a mud puddle against one wall so you could see what was going on underwater. Sometimes segment worms crawling through the reddish earth hit the side so their tunnels were visible for a few inches. In hot weather the inside of the plastic got coated with mist and droplets. The small round leaves on the litmus vines changed from blue to pink, blue to pink as clouds coursed the sky and the pH of the photosensitive soil shifted slightly.

The kids would run out before dawn and belly down naked in the cool sand with their chins on the backs of their hands and stare in the half-

dark till the red mill wheel of Sigma lifted over
the bloody sea. The sand was maroon then, and
the flowers of the crystal plants looked like rubies
in the dim light of the giant sun. Up the beach
the jungle would begin to whisper while somewhere an animal would start warbling. The kids
would giggle and poke each other and crowd
closer.

Then Sigma-prime, the second member of the
binary, would flare like thermite on the water,
and crimson clouds would bleach from coral,
through peach, to foam. The kids, half on top of
each other now, lay like a pile of copper ingots
with sun streaks in their hair—even on little
Antoni, my oldest, whose hair was black and
curly like bubbling oil (like his mother's), the
down on the small of his two-year-old back was a
white haze across the copper if you looked that
close to see.

More children came to squat and lean on their
knees, or kneel with their noses an inch from the
walls, to watch, like young magicians, as things
were born, grew, matured, and other things were
born. Enchanted at their own construction, they
stared at the miracle in their live museum.

A small, red seed lay camouflaged in the silt by
the lake/puddle. One evening as white Sigma-
prime left the sky violet, it broke open into a
brown larva as long and of the same color as the
first joint of Antoni's thumb. It flipped and
swirled in the mud a couple of days, then crawled
to the first branch of the nearest crystal plant to
hang, exhausted, head down, from the tip. The
brown flesh hardened, thickened, grew shiny,
black. Then one morning the children saw the
onyx chrysalis crack, and by second dawn there
was an emerald-eyed flying lizard buzzing at the
plastic panels.

"Oh, look, Da!" they called to me. "It's trying to get out!"

The speed-hazed creature butted at the corner for a few days, then settled at last to crawling around the broad leaves of the miniature shade palms.

When the season grew cool and there was the annual debate over whether the kids should put tunics on—they never stayed in them more than twenty minutes anyway—the jewels of the crystal plant misted, their facets coarsened, and they fell like gravel.

There were little four-cupped sloths, too, big as a six-year-old's fist. Most of the time they pressed their velvety bodies against the walls and stared longingly across the sand with their retractable eye-clusters. Then two of them swelled for about three weeks. We thought at first it was some bloating infection. But one evening there were a couple of litters of white velvet balls half hidden by the low leaves of the shade palms. The parents were occupied now and didn't pine to get out.

There was a rock half in and half out of the puddle, I remember, covered with what I'd always called mustard-moss when I saw it in the wild. Once it put out a brush of white hairs. And one afternoon the children ran to collect all the adults they could drag over. "Look! Oh Da, Da, Ma, look!" The hairs had detached themselves and were walking around the water's edge, turning end over end along the soft soil.

I had to leave for work in a few minutes and haul some spare drive parts out to Tau Ceti. But when I got back five days later, the hairs had taken root, thickened, and were already putting out the small round leaves of litmus vines. Among the new shoots, lying on her back, claws curled over her wrinkled belly, eyes cataracted like the foggy jewels of the crystal plant—she'd dropped her wings like cellophane days ago—was the flying lizard. Her pearl throat still pulsed, but as I watched, it stopped. Before she died, however, she had managed to deposit, nearly camouflaged in the silt by the puddle, a scattering of red seeds.

I remember getting home from another job where I'd been doing the maintenance on the shuttle-boats for a crew putting up a ring station to circle a planet itself circling Aldebaran. I was gone a long time on that one. When I left the landing complex and wandered out toward the tall weeds at the edge of the beach, I still didn't see anybody.

Which was just as well because the night before I'd put on a real winner with the crew to celebrate the completion of the station. That morning I'd taken a couple more drinks at the landing bar to undo last night's damage. Never works.

The swish of frond on frond was like clashed rasps. Sun on the sand reached out fingers of pure glare and tried to gouge my eyes. I was glad the home-compound was deserted because the kids would have asked questions I didn't want to answer: the adults wouldn't ask anything, which was even harder.

Then, down by the ecologarium, a child screeched. And screeched again. Then Antoni came hurtling toward me, half running, half on all fours, and flung himself on my leg. "Oh, Da! Da! Why, oh why, Da?"

I'd kicked my boots off and shrugged my shirt back at the compound porch, but I still had my overalls on. Antoni had two fists full of my pants leg and wouldn't let go. "Hey, kid-boy, what's the matter?"

When I finally got him on my shoulder he butted his blubber wet face against my collarbone. "Oh, Da! Da! It's crazy, it's all cra*aaa*-zy!" His voice rose to lose itself in sobs.

"What's crazy, kid-boy? Tell Da."

Antoni held my ear and cried while I walked down to the plastic enclosure.

They'd put a small door in one wall with a two-number combination lock that was supposed to keep this sort of thing from happening. I guess Antoni learned the combination from watching the older kids; or maybe he just figured it out.

One of the young sloths had climbed out and wandered across the sand about three feet.

"See, Da! It crazy, it bit me. Bit me, Da!" Sobs became sniffles as he showed me a puffy, bluish place on his wrist centered on which was a tiny crescent of pinpricks. Then he pointed jerkily to the creature.

It was shivering, and bloody froth spluttered from its lip flaps. All the while it was digging futilely at the sand with its clumsy cups, eyes retracted. Now it fell over, kicked, tried to right itself, breath going like a flutter valve. "It can't take the heat," I explained, reaching down to pick it up.

It snapped at me, and I jerked back. "Sunstroke, kid-boy. Yeah, it is crazy."

Suddenly it opened its mouth wide, let out all its air, and didn't take in any more. "It's all right now," I said.

Two more of the baby sloths were at the door, front cups over the sill, staring with bright, black eyes. I pushed them back with a piece of seashell and closed the door. Antoni kept looking at the white fur ball on the sand. "Not crazy now?"

"It's dead," I told him.

"Dead because it went outside, Da?"

I nodded.

"And crazy?" He made a fist and ground something already soft and wet around his upper lip.

I decided to change the subject, which was already too close to something I didn't like to think about. "Who's been taking care of you, anyway?" I asked. "You're a mess, kid-boy. Let's go and fix up that arm. They shouldn't leave a fellow your age all by himself." We started back to the compound. Those bites infect easily, and this one was swelling.

"Why it go crazy? Why it die when it go outside, Da?"

"Can't take the light," I said as we reached the jungle. "They're animals that live in shadow most of the time. The plastic cuts out the ultraviolet rays, just like the leaves that shade them when they run loose in the jungle. Sigma-prime's high on ultraviolet. That's why you're so good-looking, kid-boy. I think your ma told me their nervous systems are on the surface, all that fuzz. Under the ultra-violet, the enzymes break down so quickly that—does this mean anything to you at all?"

"Uh-uh." Antoni shook his head. Then he came out with, "Wouldn't it be nice, Da—" he admired his bite while we walked "—if some of them could go outside, just a few?"

That stopped me. There were sunspots on his blue-black hair. Fronds reflected faint green on his brown cheek. He was grinning, little, and wonderful. Something that had been anger in me a lot of times momentarily melted to raging tenderness, whirling about him like the dust in the light striking down at my shoulders, raging to protect my son. "I don't know about that, kid-boy."

"Why not?"

"It might be pretty bad for the ones who had to stay inside," I told him. "I mean after a while."

"Why?"

I started walking again. "Come on, let's fix your arm and get you cleaned up."

I washed the wet stuff off his face, and scraped the dry stuff from beneath it which had been there at least two days. Then I got some antibiotic into him.

"You smell funny, Da."

"Never mind how I smell. Let's go outside again." I put down a cup of black coffee too fast, and it and my hangover had a fight in my stomach. I tried to ignore it and do a little looking around. But I still couldn't find anybody. That got me mad. I mean he's independent, sure: he's mine. But he's only two.

Back on the beach we buried the dead sloth in sand; then I pointed out the new, glittering stalks of the tiny crystal plants. At the bottom of the pond, in the jellied mass of ani-wort eggs, you could see the tadpole forms quivering already. An orange-fringed shelf fungus had sprouted nearly eight inches since it had been just a few black spores on a pile of dead leaves two weeks back.

"Grow up," Antoni chirped with nose and fists against the plastic. "Everything grow up, and up."

"That's right."

He grinned at me. "I grow!"

"You sure as hell do."

"You grow?" Then he shook his head, twice: once to say no, and the second time because he got a kick from shaking his hair around—there was a lot of it. "You don't grow. You don't get any bigger. Why don't you grow?"

"I do too," I said indignantly. "Just very slowly."

Antoni turned around, leaned on the plastic

and moved one toe at a time in the sand—I can't do that—watching me.

"You have to grow all the time," I said. "Not necessarily get bigger. But inside your head you have to grow, kid-boy. For us human-type people that's what's important. And that kind of growing never stops. At least it shouldn't. You can grow, kid-boy, or you can die. That's the choice you've got, and it goes on all of your life."

He looked back over his shoulder. "Grow up, all the time, even if they can't get out."

"Yeah," I said. And was uncomfortable all over again. I started pulling off my overalls for something to do. "Even—" The zipper got stuck. "God *damn* it—if you can't get out." *Rnrnrnrnrn*—it came loose.

The rest got back that evening. They'd been on a group trip around the foot of the mountain. I did a little shouting to make sure my point got across about leaving Antoni alone. Didn't do much good. You know how family arguments go:

He didn't want to come. We weren't going to force—

So what. He's got to learn to do things he doesn't want—

Like some other people I could mention!

Now look—

It's a healthy group. Don't you want him to grow up a healthy—

I'll be happy if he just grows up period. No food, no medical—

But the server was chock full of food. He knows how to use it—

Look, when I got home the kid's arm was swollen all the way up to his elbow!

And so on and so forth, with Antoni sitting in the middle looking confused. When he got confused enough, he ended it all by announcing matter-of-factly: "Da smell funny when he came home."

Everyone got quiet. Then someone said, "Oh, Vyme, you didn't come home that way again! I mean, in front of the children ..."

I said a couple of things I was sorry for later and stalked off down the beach—on a four-mile hike.

Times I got home from work? The ecologarium? I guess I'm just leading up to this one.

The particular job had taken me a hectic week to get. It was putting back together a battleship that was gutted somewhere off Aurigae. Only when I got there, I found I'd already been laid off. That particular war was over—they're real quick now. So I scraped and lied and browned my way into a repair gang that was servicing a traveling replacement station, generally had to humiliate myself to get the job because every other drive mechanic from the battleship fiasco was after it too. Then I got canned the first day because I came to work smelling funny. It took me another week to hitch a ride back to Sigma. Didn't even have enough to pay passage, but I made a deal with the pilot I'd do half the driving for him.

We were an hour out, and I was at the controls when something I'd never heard of happening, happened. We came *this* close to ramming another ship. Consider how much empty space there is; the chances are infinitesimal. And on top of that, every ship should be broadcasting an identification beam at all times.

But this big, bulbous keeler-intergalactic slid by so close I could *see* her through the front viewport. Our inertia system went nuts. We jerked around in the stasis whirl from the keeler. I slammed on the video-intercom and shouted, "You great big stupid ... *stupid* ..." so mad and scared I couldn't say anything else.

The golden piloting the ship stared at me from the view-screen with mildly surprised annoyance. I remember his face was just slightly more Negroid than mine.

Our little Serpentina couldn't hurt him. But had we been even a hundred meters closer we might have ionized. The other pilot came bellowing from behind the sleeper curtain and started cursing me-out.

"Damn it," I shouted, "it was one of those . . ." and lost all the profanity I know to my rage, ". . . golden . . ."

"This far into galactic center? Come off it. They should be hanging out around the Star-pit!"

"It was a keeler drive," I insisted. "It came right in front of us." I stopped because the control stick was shaking in my hand. You know the Serpentina colophon? They have it in the corner of the view-screen and raised in plastic on the head of the control knobs. Well, it got pressed into the ham of my thumb so you could make it out for an hour, I was squeezing the control rod that tight.

When he set me down, I went straight to the bar to cool off. And got in a fight. When I reached the beach I was broke, I had a bloody nose, I was sick, and furious.

It was just after first sunset, and the kids were squealing around the ecologarium. Then one little girl I didn't even recognize ran up to me and jerked my arm. "Da, oh, Da! Come look! The ani-worts are just about to—"

I pushed her, and she sat down, surprised, on the sand.

I just wanted to get to the water and splash something cold on my face, because every minute or so it would start to burn.

Another bunch of kids grabbed me, shouting, "Da, Da, the ani-worts, Da!" and tried to pull me over.

First I took two steps with them. Then I just swung my arms out. I didn't make a sound. But I put my head down and barreled against the plastic wall. Kids screamed. Aluminum snapped; the plastic cracked and went down. My boots were still on, and I kicked and kicked at red earth and sand. Shade palms went down and the leaves tore under my feet. Crystal plants broke like glass rods beneath a piece of plastic. A swarm of lizards flittered up around my head. Some of the red was Sigma, some was what burned behind my face.

I remember I was still shaking and watching water run out of the broken lake over the sand, then soak in so that the wet tongue of sand expanded a little, raised just a trifle around the edge. Then I looked up to see the kids coming back down the beach, crying, shouting, afraid and clustered around Antoni's ma. She walked steadily toward me—steady because she was a woman and they were children. But I saw the same fear in her face. Antoni was on her shoulder. Other grown-ups were coming behind her.

Antoni's ma was a biologist, and I think she had suggested the ecologarium to the kids in the first place. When she looked up from the ruin I'd made, I knew I'd broken something of hers too.

An odd expression got caught in the features of her—I remember it oh so beautiful—face, with compassion alongside the anger, contempt alongside the fear. "Oh, for pity's sake, Vyme," she cried, not loudly at all. "Won't you ever grow up?"

I opened my mouth, but everything I wanted to say was too big and stayed wedged in my throat.

"Grow up?" Antoni repeated and reached for a lizard that buzzed his head. "Everything stop growing up, now." He looked down again at the wreck I'd made. "All broken. Everything get out."

"He didn't mean to break it," she said to the others for me, then knifed my gratitude with a look. "We'll put it back together."

She put Antoni on the sand and picked up one of the walls.

After they got started, they let me help. A lot of the plants were broken. And only the ani-worts who'd completed metamorphosis could be saved. The flying lizards were too curious to get far away, so we—they netted them and got them back inside. I guess I didn't help that much. And I wouldn't say I was sorry.

They got just about everything back except the sloths.

We couldn't find them. We searched for a long time, too.

The sun was down so they should have been all right. They can't negotiate the sand with any speed so couldn't have reached the jungle. But there were no tracks, no nothing. We even dug in the sand to see if they'd buried themselves. It wasn't till more than a dozen years later I discovered where they went.

For the present I accepted Antoni's mildly adequate, "They just must of got out again."

Not too long after that I left the procreation group. Went off to work one day, didn't come back. But like I said to Antoni, you either grow or die. I didn't die.

Once I considered returning. But there was another war, and suddenly there wasn't anything to return to. Some of the group got out alive. Antoni and his ma didn't. I mean there wasn't even any water left on the planet.

When I finally came to the Star-pit, myself, I hadn't had a drink in years. But working there out on the galaxy's edge did something to me—

something to the part that grows I'd once talked about on the beach with Antoni.

If it did it to me, it's not surprising it did it to Ratlit and the rest.

(And I remember a black-eyed creature pressed against the plastic wall, staring across impassable sands.)

Perhaps it was knowing this was as far as you could go.

Perhaps it was the golden.

Golden? I hadn't even joined the group yet when I first heard the word. I was sixteen and a sophomore at Luna Vocational. I was born in a city called New York on a planet called Earth. Luna is its one satellite. You've heard of the system, I'm sure; that's where we all came from. A few other things about it are well known. Unless you're an anthropologist, though, I doubt you've ever been there. It's way the hell off the main trading routes and pretty primitive. I was a drive-mechanics major, on scholarship, living in and studying hard. All morning in Practical Theory (a ridiculous name for a ridiculous class, I thought then) we'd been putting together a model keeler-intergalactic drive. Throughout those dozens of helical inserts and superinertia organus sensitives, I had been silently cursing my teacher, thinking, about like everyone else in the class, "So what if they can fly these jalopies from one galaxy to another. Nobody will ever be able to ride in them. Not with the Psychic and Physiologic shells hanging around this cluster of the universe."

Back in the dormitory I was lying on my bed, scraping graphite lubricant from my nails with the end of my slide rule and half reading at a folded-back copy of *The Young Mechanic* when I saw the article and the pictures.

Through some freakish accident, two people

had been discovered who didn't crack up at twenty thousand light-years off the galactic rim, who didn't die at twenty-five thousand.

They were both psychological freaks with some incredible hormone imbalance in their systems. One was a little Oriental girl; the other was an older man, blond and big-boned, from a cold planet circling Cygnus-beta: golden. They looked sullen as hell, both of them.

Then there were more articles, more pictures, in the economic journals, the sociology student-letters, the legal bulletins, as various fields began acknowledging the impact that the golden and the sudden birth of intergalactic trade were having on them. The head of some commission summed it up with the statement: "Though interstellar travel has been with us for three centuries, intergalactic trade has been an impossibility, not because of mechanical limitations, but rather because of barriers that till now we have not even been able to define. Some psychic shock causes insanity in any human—or for that matter, any intelligent species or perceptual machine or computer—that goes more than twenty thousand light-years from the galactic rim; then complete physiological death, as well as recording break-down in computers that might replace human crews. Complex explanations have been offered, none completely satisfactory, but the base of the problem seems to be this: as the nature of space and time are relative to the concentration of matter in a given area of the continuum, the nature of reality itself operates by the same, or similar laws. The averaged mass of all the stars in our galaxy controls the 'reality' of our micro-sector of the universe. But as a ship leaves the galactic rim, 'reality' breaks down and causes insanity and eventual death for any crew, even

though certain mechanical laws—though not all—
appear to remain, for reasons we don't understand, relatively constant. Save for a few barbaric
experiments done with psychedelics at the dawn
of spatial travel, we have not even developed a
vocabulary that can deal with 'reality' apart from
its measurable, physical expression. Yet, just when
we had to face the black limit of intergalactic
space, bright resources glittered within. Some
few of us whose sense of reality has been shattered by infantile, childhood, or prenatal trauma,
whose physiological orientation makes life in our
interstellar society painful or impossible—not all,
but a few of these golden ..." at which point
there was static, or the gentleman coughed, "...
can make the crossing and return."

The name golden, sans noun, stuck.

Few was the understatement of the millennium.
Slightly less than one human being in thirty-four
thousand is a golden. A couple of people had
pictures of emptying all mental institutions by
just shaking them out over the galactic rim.
Didn't work like that. The particular psychosis
and endocrine setup was remarkably specialized.
Still, back then there was excitement, wonder,
anticipation, hope, admiration in the word: admiration for the ones who could get out.

"Golden?" Ratlit said when I asked him. He
was working as a grease monkey out here in the
Star-pit over at Poloscki's. "Born with the word.
Grew up with it. Weren't no first time with me.
Though I remember when I was about six, right
after the last of my parents was killed, and I was
hiding out with a bunch of other lice in a
broke-open packing crate in an abandoned freight
yard near the ruins of Helios on Creton VII—
that's where I was born, I think. Most of the city
had been starved out by then, but somebody was

getting food to us. There was this old crook-back character who was hiding too. He used to sit on the top of the packing crate and bang his heels on the aluminum slats and tell us stories about the stars. Had a couple of rags held with twists of wire for clothes, missing two fingers off one hand; he kept plucking the loose skin under his chin with those grimy talons. And he talked about them. So I asked, 'Golden what, sir?' He leaned forward so that his face was like a mahogany bruise on the sky, and croaked. 'They've been *out*, I tell you, seen more than ever you or I. Human and inhuman, kid-boy, mothered by women and fathered by men, still they live by their own laws and walk their own ways!' " Ratlit and I were sitting under a street lamp with our feet over the Edge where the fence had broken. His hair was like breathing flame in the wind; his single earring glittered. Star-flecked infinity dropped away below our boot soles, and the wind created by the stasis field that held our atmosphere down—we call it the "world-wind" out here because it's never cold and never hot and like nothing on any world—whipped his black shirt back from his bony chest as we gazed on galactic night between our knees. "I guess that was back during the second Kyber war," he concluded.

"Kyber war?" I asked. "Which one was that?"

He shrugged. "I just know it was fought over possession of couple of tons of di-allium; that's the polarized element the golden brought back from Lupe-galaxy. They used y-adna ships to fight it—that's why it was such a bad one. I mean worse than usual."

"Y-adna? That's a drive I don't know anything about."

"Some golden saw the plans for them in a civilization in Magellanic-9."

"Oh," I said. "And what was Kyber?"

"It was a weapon, a sort of fungus the golden brought back from some overrun planet on the rim of Andromeda. It's deadly. Only they were too stupid to bring back the antitoxin."

"That's golden for you."

"Yeah. You ever notice about golden, Vyme? I mean just the word. I found out all about it from my publisher, once. It's semantically unsettling."

"Really?" I said. "So are they. Unsettling I mean."

I'd just finished a rough, rough day installing a rebuilt keeler in a quantum transport hull that just wasn't big enough. The golden having the job done stood over my shoulder the whole time, and every hour he'd come out with the sort of added instruction that would make the next sixty-one minutes miserable. But I did it. The golden paid me in cash and without a word climbed into the lift, and two minutes later, while I was still washing the grease off, the damn five-hundred-ton hulk began to whistle for takeoff.

Sandy, a young fellow who'd come looking for a temporary mechanic's job three months back, but hadn't given me cause to fire him yet, barely had time to pull the big waldoes out of the way and go scooting into the shock chamber when the three-hundred-meter doofus tore loose from the grapplers. And Sandy, who, like a lot of these youngsters drifting around from job to job, is usually sort of quiet and vague, got loud and specific. " . . . two thousand pounds of nonshockproof equipment out there . . . ruin it all if he could . . . *I'm* not expendable, I don't care what a . . . these golden out here . . ." while the ship hove off where only the golden go. I just flipped on the "not-open" sign, left the rest of the grease where it was, left the hanger, and hunted up Ratlit.

So there we were, under that street lamp, sitting on the Edge, in the world-wind.

"Golden," Ratlit said under the roar. "It would be much easier to take if it were grammatically connected to something: golden ones, golden people. Or even one gold, two golden."

"Male golden, female goldene?"

"Something like that. It's not an adjective, it's not a noun. My publisher told me that for a while it was written with a dash after it that stood for whatever it might modify."

I remembered the dash. It was an uneasy joke, a fill-in for that cough. Golden *what?* People had already started to feel uncomfortable. Then it went past joking and back to just "golden."

"Think about that, Vyme. Just golden: one, two, or three of them."

"That's something to think about, kid-boy," I said.

Ratlit had been six during the Kyber war. Square that and add it once again for my age now. Ratlit's? Double six and add one. I like kids; and they like me. But that may be because my childhood left me a lot younger at forty-two than I should be. Ratlit's had left him a lot older than any thirteen-year-old has a right to be.

"No golden took part in the war," Ratlit said.

"They never do." I watched his thin fingers get all tangled together.

After two divorces, my mother ran off with a salesman and left me and four siblings with an alcoholic aunt for a year. Yeah, they still have divorces, monogamous marriages and stuff like that where I was born. Like I say, it's pretty primitive. I left home at fifteen, made it through vocational school on my own, and learned enough about what makes things fly to end up—after that disastrous marriage I told you about earlier—with my own repair hangar on the Star-pit.

Compared with Ratlit I had a stable childhood.

That's right, he lost the last parent he remembered when he was six. At seven he was convicted of his first felony—after escaping from Creton VII. But part of his treatment at hospital *cum* reform school *cum* prison was to have the details lifted from his memory. "Did something to my head back there. That's why I never could learn to read, I think." For the next couple of years he ran away from one foster group after the other. When he was eleven, some guy took him home from Play Planet where he'd been existing under the boardwalk on discarded hot dogs, souvlakia, and falafel. "Fat, smoked perfumed cigarettes; name was Vivian?" Turned out to be the publisher. Ratlit stayed for three months, during which time he dictated a novel to Vivian. "Protecting my honor," Ratlit explained. "I had to do *something* to keep him busy."

The book sold a few hundred thousand copies as a precocious curiosity among many. But Ratlit had split. The next years he was involved as a shill in some illegality I never understood. He didn't either. "But I bet I made a million, Vyme! I earned at least a million." It's possible. At thirteen he still couldn't read or write, but his travels had gained him fair fluency in three languages. A couple of weeks ago he'd wandered off a stellar tramp, dirty and broke, here at the Star-pit. And I'd gotten him a job as grease monkey over at Poloscki's.

He leaned his elbows on his knees, his chin in his hands. "Vyme, it's a shame."

"What's a shame, kid-boy?"

"To be washed up at my age. A has-been! To

have to grapple with the fact that this—" he spat
at a star "—is it."

He was talking about golden again.

"You still have a chance." I shrugged. "Most of
the time it doesn't come out till puberty."

He cocked his head up at me. "I've been
pubescent since I was nine, buster."

"Ex*cuse* me."

"I feel cramped in, Vyme. There's all that night
out there to grow up in, to explore."

"There was a time," I mused, "when the whole
species was confined to the surface, give or take a
few feet up or down, of a single planet. You've
got the whole galaxy to run around in. You've
seen a lot of it, yeah. But not all."

"But there are billions of galaxies out there. I
want to see them. In all the stars around here
there hasn't been one life form discovered that's
based on anything but silicon or carbon. I over-
heard two golden in a bar once, talking: there's
something in some galaxy out there that's big as
a star, neither dead nor alive, and sings. I want to
hear it, Vyme!"

"Ratlit, you can't fight reality."

"Oh, go to sleep, grandpa!" He closed his eyes
and bent his head back until the cords of his neck
quivered. "What is it that makes a golden? A
combination of physiological and psychological
. . . what?"

"It's primarily some sort of hormonal imbalance as well as an environmentally conditioned
thalamic/personality response—"

"Yeah. Yeah." His head came down. "And that
X-chromosome heredity nonsense they just connected
up with it a few years back. But all I know is
they can take the stasis shift from galaxy to galaxy,
where you and I, Vyme, if we get more than twenty
thousand light-years off the rim, we're dead."

"Insane at twenty thousand," I corrected. "Dead at twenty-five."

"Same difference." He opened his eyes. They were large, green, and mostly pupil. "You know, I stole a golden belt once? Rolled it off a staggering slob about a week ago who came out of a bar and collapsed on the corner. I went across the Pit to the Calle-J where nobody knows me and wore it around for a few hours, just to see if I felt different."

"You did?" Ratlit had lengths of gut that astounded me about once a day.

"I didn't. But people walking around me did. Wearing that two-inch band of yellow metal around my waist, nobody in the worlds could tell I wasn't a golden, just walking by on the street, without talking to me awhile, or making hormone tests. And wearing that belt, I learned just how much I hated golden. Because I could suddenly see, in almost everybody who came by, how much they hated me while I had that metal belt on. I threw it over the Edge." Suddenly he grinned. "Maybe I'll steal another one."

"You really hate them, Ratlit?"

He narrowed his eyes at me and looked superior.

"Sure, I talk about them," I told him. "Sometimes they're a pain to work for. But it's not their fault we can't take the reality shift."

"I'm just a child," he said evenly, "incapable of such fine reasoning. I hate them." He looked back at the night. "How can you stand to be trapped by anything, Vyme?"

Three memories crowded into my head when he said that.

First: I was standing at the railing of the East River—runs past this New York I was telling you about—at midnight, looking at the illuminated dragon of the Manhattan Bridge that spanned the water, then at the industrial fires flickering in bright, smoky Brooklyn, and then at the template of mercury street lamps behind me bleaching out the playground and most of Houston Street; then, at the reflections in the water, here like crinkled foil, there like glistening rubber; at last, looked up at the midnight sky itself. It wasn't black but dead pink, without a star. This glittering world made the sky a roof that pressed down on me so I almost screamed. . . . That time the next night I was twenty-seven light-years away from Sol on my first star-run.

Second: I was visiting my mother after my first few years out. I was looking in the closet for something when this contraption of plastic straps and buckles fell on my head.

"What's this, Ma?"

And she smiled with a look of idiot nostalgia and crooned, "Why that's your little harness, Vymey. Your first father and I would take you on picnics up at Bear Mountain and put you in that and tie you to a tree with about ten foot of cord so you wouldn't get—" I didn't hear the rest because of the horror that suddenly flooded me, thinking of myself tied up in that thing. Okay, I was twenty and had just joined that beautiful procreation group a year back on Sigma and was the proud father of three and expecting two more. The hundred and sixty-three of us had the whole beach and nine miles of jungle and half a mountain to ourselves; maybe I was seeing Antoni caught up in that thing, trying to catch a bird or a beetle or a wave—with only ten feet of cord. I hadn't worn clothes for anything but work in a twelvemonth, and I was chomping to get away from the incredible place I had grown up in called an apartment and back to wives, husbands, kids, and civilization. Anyway, it was pretty terrible.

The third? After I had left the proke-group—
fled them, I suppose, guilty and embarrassed over
something I couldn't name, still having night-
mares once a month that woke me screaming
about what was going to happen to the kids, even
though I knew one point of group marriage was
to prevent the loss of one, two, or three parents
being traumatic—still wondering if I wasn't making the same mistakes my parents made, hoping
my brood wouldn't turn out like me, or worse
like the kids you sometimes read about in the
paper (like Ratlit, though I hadn't met him yet),
horribly suspicious that no matter how different I
tried to be from my sires, it was just the same
thing all over again. . . . Anyway, I was on the
ship bringing me to the Star-pit for the first time.
I'd gotten talking to a golden who, as golden go,
was a pretty regular gal. We'd been discussing
inter- and intra-galactic drives. She was impressed I knew so much. I was impressed that she
could use them and know so little. She was
digging in a very girl-way the six-foot-four, two-
hundred-and-ten-pound drive mechanic with mildly
grimy fingernails and that was me. I was digging
in a very boy-way the slim, amber-eyed young
lady who had seen it *all*. From the view deck we
watched the immense, artificial disk of the Star-
pit approach, when she turned to me and said, in
a voice that didn't sound cruel at all, "This is as
far as you go, isn't it?" And I was frightened all
over again, because I knew that on about nine
different levels she was right.

Ratlit said: "I know what you're thinking." A
couple of times when he'd felt like being quiet
and I'd felt like talking I may have told him more
than I should. "Well, cube that for me, dad.
That's how trapped I feel!"

I laughed, and Ratlit looked very young again.
"Come on," I said. "Let's take a walk."

"Yeah." He stood. The wind fingered at our
hair. "I want to go see Alegra."

"I'll walk you as far as Calle-G," I told him.
"Then I'm going to go to bed."

"I wonder what Alegra thinks about this business? I always find Alegra a very good person to
talk to," he said sagely. "Not to put you down,
but her experiences are a little more up to date
than yours. You have to admit she has a modern
point of view. Plus the fact that she's older."
Than Ratlit anyway. She was fifteen.

"I don't think being 'trapped' ever really bothered her," I said. "Which may be a place to take
a lesson from."

By Ratlit's standards Alegra had a few things
over me. In my youth kids took to dope in their
teens, twenties. Algera was born with a three-
hundred-milligram-a-day habit on a bizarre nar-
cotic that combined the psychedelic qualities of
the most powerful hallucinogens with the addic-
tiveness of the strongest depressants. I can sym-
pathize. Alegra's mother was addicted, and the
tolerance was passed with the blood plasma
through the placental wall. Ordinarily a couple of
complete transfusions at birth would have gotten
the newborn child straight. But Alegra was also a
highly projective telepath. She projected the hor-
rors of birth, the glories of her infantile halluci-
nated world on befuddled doctors; she was given
her drug. Without too much difficulty she managed to be given her drug every day since.

Once I asked Alegra when she'd first heard of
the golden, and she came back with this horror
story. A lot were coming back from Tiber-44
cluster with psychic shock—the mental condition
of golden is pretty delicate, and sometimes very

minor conflicts nearly ruin them. Anyway, the government that was sponsoring the importation of micro-micro surgical equipment from some tiny planet in that galaxy, to protect its interests, hired Alegra, age eight, as a psychiatric therapist. "I'd concretize their fantasies and make them work them through. In just a couple of hours I'd have 'em back to their old, mean, stupid selves again. Some of them were pretty nice when they came to me." But there was a lot of work for her; projective telepaths are rare. So they started withholding her drug to force her to work harder, then rewarding her with increased dosage. "Up till then," she told me, "I might have kicked it. But when I came away, they had me on double what I used to take. They pushed me past the point where withdrawal would be fatal. But I *could* have kicked it, up till then, Vyme." That's right. Age eight.

Oh yeah. The drug was imported by golden from Cancer-9 and most of it goes through the Star-pit. Alegra came here because illegal imports are easier to come by, and you can get it for just about nothing—if you want it. Golden don't use it.

The wind lessened as Ratlit and I started back. Ratlit began to whistle. In Calle-K the first night lamp had broken so that the level street was a tunnel of black.

"Ratlit?" I asked. "Where do you think you'll be, oh, in say five years?"

"Quiet," he said. "I'm trying to get to the end of the street without bumping into the walls, tripping on something, or some other catastrophe. If we get through the next five minutes all right, I'll worry about the next five years." He began whistling again.

"Trip? Bump the walls?"

"I'm listening for echoes." Again he commenced the little jets of music.

I put my hands in my overall pouch and went on quietly while Ratlit did the bat bit. Then there was a catastrophe. Though I didn't realize it at the time.

Into the circle of light from the remaining lamp at the other end of the street walked a golden.

His hands went up to his face, and he was laughing. The sound skittered in the street. His belt was low on his belly the way the really down and broke—

I just thought of a better way to describe him; the resemblance struck me immediately. He looked like Sandy, my mechanic, who is short, twenty-four years old, muscled like an ape, and wears his worn-out work clothes even when he's off duty. ("I just want this job for a while, boss. I'm not staying out here at the Star-pit. As soon as I save up a little, I'm gonna make it back in toward galactic center. It's funny out here, like dead." He gazes up through the opening in the hangar roof where there are no clouds and no stars either. "Yeah. I'm just gonna be here for a little while.")

("Fine with me, kid-boy.")

(That was three months back, like I say. He's still with me. He works hard too, which puts him a cut above a lot of characters out here. Still, there was something about Sandy . . .) On the other hand Sandy's face is also hacked up with acne. His hair is always nap short over his wide head. But in these aspects, the golden was exactly Sandy's opposite, come to think of it. Still, there was something about the golden . . .

He staggered, went down on his knees still laughing, then collapsed. By the time we reached him, he was silent. With the toe of his boot Ratlit nudged the hand from the belt buckle.

It flopped, palm up, on the pavement. The little fingernail was three quarters of an inch long, the way a lot of the golden wear it. (Like his face, the tips of Sandy's fingers are all masticated wrecks. Still, something . . .)

"Now isn't that something." Ratlit shook his head. "What do you want to do with him, Vyme?"

"Nothing," I said. "Let him sleep it off."

"Leave him so somebody can come along and steal his belt?" Ratlit grinned. "I'm not that nasty."

"Weren't you just telling me how much you hated golden?"

"I'd be nasty to whoever stole the belt and wore it. Nobody but a golden should be hated that much."

"Ratlit, let's go."

But he had already kneeled down and was shaking the golden's shoulder. "Let's get him to Alegra's and find out what's the matter with him."

"He's just drunk."

"Nope," Ratlit said. "Cause he don't smell funny."

"Look. Get back." I hoisted the golden up and laid him across my neck, fireman's carry. "Start moving," I told Ratlit. "I think you're crazy."

Ratlit grinned. "Thanks. Maybe he'll be grateful and lay some lepta on me for taking him in off the street."

"You don't know golden," I said. "But if he does, split it with me."

"Sure."

Two blocks later we reached Alegra's place. (But like I say, Sandy, though well built, is little; so I didn't have much trouble carrying him.) Halfway up the tilting stairs Ratlit said, "She's in a good mood."

"I guess she is." The weight across my shoulders was becoming pleasant.

I can't describe Alegra's place. I can describe a lot of places like it; and I can describe it before she moved in because I knew a derelict named Drunk-roach who slept on that floor before she did. You know what never-wear plastics look like when they wear out? What nonrust metals look like when they rust through? It was a shabby crack-walled cubicle with dirt in the corners and scars on the windowpane when Drunk-roach had his pile of blankets in the corner. But since the hallucinating projective telepath took it over, who knows what it had become.

Ratlit opened the door on an explosion of classical beauty.

"Come in," she said, accompanied by symphonic arrangement scored on twenty-four staves, with full chorus. "What's that you're carrying, Vyme? Oh, it's a golden!"

And before me, dizzying tides of yellow.

"Put him down, put him down quick and let's see what's wrong!"

Hundreds of eyes, spotlights, glittering lenses; I lowered him to the mattress in the corner.

"Ohhh ..." breathed Alegra.

And the golden lay on orange silk pillows in a teak barge drawn by swans, accompanied by flutes and drums.

"Where did you find him?" she hissed, circling against the ivory moon on her broom.

We watched the glowing barge, hundreds of feet below, sliding down the silvered waters between the crags.

"We just picked him up off the street," Ratlit said. "Vyme thought he was drunk. But he don't smell."

"Was he laughing?" Alegra asked.

Laughter rolled and broke on the rocks.

"Yeah," Ratlit said. "Just before he collapsed."

"Then he must be from the Un-dok expedition that just got back."

Mosquitoes darted at us through wet fronds. The insects reeled among the leaves, upsetting droplets that fell like glass as, barely visible beyond the palms, the barge drifted on the bright, sweltering river.

"That's right," I said, backpaddling frantically to avoid a hippopotamus that threatened to upset my kayak. "I'd forgotten they'd just come in."

"Okay," Ratlit's breath clouded his lips. "I'm out of it. Let me in. Where did they come back from?"

The snow hissed beneath the runners, as we looked after the barge, nearly at the white horizon.

"Un-dok, of course," Alegra said. The barking grew fainter. "Where did you think?"

White eclipsed to black, and the barge was a spot gleaming in galactic night, flown on by laboring comets.

"Un-dok is the furthest galaxy reached yet," I told Ratlit. "They just got back last week."

"Sick," Alegra added.

I dug my fingers against my abdomen to grab the pain.

"They all came back sick—"

Fever heated blood-bubbles in my eyes: I slipped to the ground, my mouth wide, my tongue like paper on my lips . . .

Ratlit coughed. "All *right*, Alegra. Cut it out! You don't have to be so dramatic!"

"Oh, I'm dreadfully sorry Ratty, Vyme."

Coolth, water. Nausea swept away as solicitous nurses hastily put the pieces back together until everything was beautiful, or so austerely horrible it could be appreciated as beauty.

"Anyway," she went on, "they came back with some sort of disease they picked up out there. Apparently it's not contagious, but they're stuck with it for the rest of their lives. Every few days they suddenly have a blackout. It's preceded by a fit of hysterics. It's just one of those stupid things they can't do anything about yet. It doesn't hurt their being golden."

Ratlit began to laugh. Suddenly he asked, "How long are they passed out for?"

"Only a few hours." Alegra said. "It must be terribly annoying."

And I began to feel mildly itchy in all sorts of unscratchable places, my shoulder blades, somewhere down my ear, the roof of my mouth. Have you ever tried to scratch the roof of your mouth?

"Well," Ratlit said, "let's sit down and wait it out."

"We can talk," Alegra said, patly. "That way it won't seem like such a long ..." and hundreds of years later she finished "... time."

"Good," Ratlit said. "I wanted to talk to you. That's why I came up here in the first place!"

"Oh, fine!" Alegra said. "I love to talk. I want to talk about love. Loving someone" (an incredible yearning twisted my stomach, rose to block my throat) "I mean really loving someone" (the yearning brushed the edge of agony) "means you are willing to admit the person you love is not what you first fell in love with, not the image you first had; and you must be able to like them still for being as close to that image as they are, and avoid disliking them for being so far away."

And through the tenderness that suddenly obliterated all hurt, Ratlit's voice came from the jeweled mosaics shielding him: "Alegra, I want to talk about loneliness."

"I'm on my way home, kids," I said. "Tell me

what happens with Prince Charming when he wakes up." They kept on talking while I went through the difficulties of finding my way out without Alegra's help. When my head cleared, halfway down the stairs, I couldn't tell you if I'd been there five minutes or five years.

When I got to the hangar next morning Sandy was filing the eight-foot prongs on the conveyor. "You got a job coming in about twenty minutes," he called down from the scaffold.

"I hope it's not another of those rebuilt jobs."

"Yep."

"Hell," I said. "I don't want to see another one for six weeks."

"All he wants is a general tune-up. Maybe two hours."

"Depends on where it's been," I said. "Where *has* it been?"

"Just back from—"

"Never mind." I started toward the office cubicle. "I think I'll put the books in order for the last six months. Can't let it go forever."

"Boss!" Sandy protested. "That'll take all day!"

"Then I better get started." I leaned back out the door. "Don't disturb me."

Of course as soon as the shadow of the hull fell over the office window I came out in my overalls, after giving Sandy five minutes to get it grappled and himself worried. I took the lift up to the one-fifty catwalk. When I stepped out, Sandy threw me a grateful smile from his scar-ugly face. The golden had already started his instructions. When I reached them and coughed, the golden turned to me and continued talking, not bothering to fill me in on what he had said before, figuring Sandy and I would put it together. You could tell this golden had made his pile. He wore an immaculate blue tunic, with bronze codpiece, bracelets and earrings. His hair was the same bronze, his skin was burned red-black, and his blue-gray eyes and tight-muscled mouth were proud, proud, proud. While I finished getting instructions, Sandy quietly got started unwelding the eight-foot seal of the organum so we could get to the checkout circuits.

Finally the golden stopped talking—that's the only way you could tell he was finished—and leaned his angular six and a half feet against the railing, clicking his glossy, manicured nails against the pipe a few times. He had that same sword-length pinky nail, all white against his skin. I climbed out on the rigging to help Sandy.

We had been at work ten minutes when a kid, maybe eighteen or nineteen, barefoot and brown, black hair hacked off shoulder length, a rag that didn't fit tucked around under his belt, and dirty, came wandering down the catwalk. His thumbs were rubbing the yellow metal links: golden.

First I thought he'd come from the ship. Then I realized he'd just stalked into the hangar from outside and come up on the lift.

"Hey, brother!" The kid who was golden hooked his thumbs in his belt, as Sandy and I watched the dialogue from the rigging on the side of the hull. "I'm getting tired of hanging around this Star-pit. Just about broke as well. Where you running to?"

The man who was golden clicked his nails again. "Go away, distant cousin."

"Come on, brother, give me a berth on your lifeboat out of this dungheap to someplace worthwhile."

"Go away, or I'll kill you."

"Now, brother, I'm just a youngster adrift in this forsaken quarter of the sky. Come on, now—"

Suddenly the blond man whirled from the railing, grabbed up a four-foot length of pipe leaning beside him, and swung it so hard it hissed. The black-haired ragamuffin leapt back and from under his rag snatched something black that, with a flick of that long nail, grew seven inches of blade. The bar swung again, caught the shoulder of the boy, then clattered against the hull. He shrieked and came straight forward. The two bodies locked, turned, fell. A gurgle, and the man's hands slipped from the neck of the ragamuffin. The boy scrambled back to his feet. Blood bubbled and popped on the hot blade.

A last spasm caught the man; he flipped over, smearing the catwalk, rolled once more, this time under the rail, and dropped—two hundred and fifty feet to the cement flooring.

Flick. Off went the power in the knife. The golden wiped powdered blood on his thigh, spat over the rail and said softly, "No relative of mine." Flick. The blade itself disappeared. He started down the catwalk.

"Hey!" Sandy called, when he got his voice back up into his throat, "what about ... I mean you ... well, your ship!" There are no familial inheritance laws among golden—only rights of plunder.

The golden glanced back. "I give it to you," he sneered. His shoulder must have been killing him, but he stepped into the lift like he was walking into a phone booth. That's a golden for you.

Sandy was horrified and bewildered. Behind his pitted ugliness there was that particularly wretched amazement only the totally vulnerable get when hurt.

"That's the first time you've ever seen an incident like that?" I felt sorry for him.

"Well, I wandered into Greg's Bar a couple of

hours after they had that massacre. But the ones who started it were drunk."

"Drunk or sober," I said. "Believe me, it doesn't mean that much difference to the way a man acts." I shook my head. "I keep forgetting you've only been here three months."

Sandy, upset, looked down at the body on the flooring. "What about him? And the ship, boss?"

"I'll call the wagon to come scrape him up. The ship is yours."

"Huh?"

"He gave it to you. It'll stand up in court. It just takes one witness. Me."

"What am I gonna do with it? I mean I would have to haul it to a junk station to get the salvage. Look, boss, I'm gonna give it to you. Sell it or something. I'd feel sort of funny with it anyway."

"I don't want it. Besides, then I'd be involved in the transaction and couldn't be a witness."

"I'll be a witness." Ratlit stepped from the lift. "I caught the whole bit when I came in the door. Great acoustics in this place." He whistled again. The echo came back. Ratlit closed his eyes for a moment. "Ceiling is . . . a hundred and twenty feet overhead, more or less. How's that, huh?"

"Hundred and twenty-seven," I said.

Ratlit shrugged. "I need more practice. Come on, Sandy, you give it to him, and I'll be a witness."

"You're a minor," Sandy said. Sandy didn't like Ratlit. I used to think it was because Ratlit was violent and flamboyant where Sandy was stolid and ugly. Even though Sandy kept protesting the temporariness of his job to me, I remember, when I first got to the Star-pit, those long-dying thoughts I'd had about leaving. It was a little too easy to see Sandy a mechanic here thirty years from now. I wasn't the only one it had happened to. Ratlit had been a grease monkey here three weeks. You tell me where he was going to be in three more. "Aren't you supposed to be working at Poloscki's?" Sandy said, turning back to the organum.

"Coffee break," Ratlit said. "If you're going to give it away, Sandy, can I have it?"

"So you can claim salvage? Hell, no!"

"I don't want it for salvage. I want it for a present." Sandy looked up again. "Yeah. To give to someone else. Finish the tune-up and give it to me, okay?"

"You're nuts, kid-boy," Sandy said. "Even if I gave you the ship, what you gonna pay for the work with?"

"Aw, it'll only take a couple of hours. You're half done anyway. I figured you'd throw in the tune-up along with it. If you really want the money, I'll get it to you a little at a time. Vyme, what sort of professional discount will you give me? I'm just a grease monkey, but I'm still in the business."

I whacked the back of his red head between a-little-too-playfully and not-too-hard. "Come on, kid-boy," I said. "Help me take care of puddles downstairs. Sandy, finish it up, huh?"

Sandy grunted and plunged both hands back into the organum.

As soon as the lift door closed, Ratlit demanded, "You gonna give it to me, Vyme?"

"It's Sandy's ship," I said.

"You tell him, and he will."

I laughed. "You tell me how your golden turned out when he came to. I assume that's who you want the ship for. What sort of fellow was he?"

Ratlit hooked his fingers in the mesh wall of

the lift cage and leaned back. "They're only two types of golden." He began to swing from side to side. "Mean ones and stupid ones." He was repeating a standard line around the Star-pit.

"I hope yours is stupid," I said, thinking of the two who'd just ruined Sandy's day and upset mine.

"Which is worse?" Ratlit shrugged. That is the rest of the line. When a golden isn't being outright mean, he exhibits the sort of nonthinkingness that gets other people hurt—you remember the one that nearly rammed my ship, or the ones who didn't bother to bring back the Kyber antitoxin? "But this one—" Ratlit stood up "—is unbelievably stupid."

"Yesterday you hated them. Today you want to give one a ship?"

"He doesn't have one," Ratlit explained calmly, as though that warranted all change of attitude. "And because he's sick, it'll be hard for him to find work unless he has one of his own."

"I see." We bounced on the silicon cushion. I pushed open the door and started for the office. "What all went on after I left? I must have missed the best part of the evening."

"You did. Will I really need that much more sleep when I pass thirty-five?"

"Cut the cracks and tell me what happened."

"Well—" Ratlit leaned against the office door jamb while I dialed narcotics. "Alegra and I talked a little after you left, till finally we realized the golden was awake and listening. Then he told us we were beautiful."

I raised an eyebrow. "Mmmm?"

"That's what we said. And he said it again, that watching us talk and think and build was one of the most beautiful things he'd ever seen. 'What have you seen?' we asked him. And he began to tell us." Ratlit stopped breathing, something built up, then, at once, it came out: "Oh, Vyme, the places he's been! The things he's done! The landscapes he's starved in, the hells where he's had to lie down and go to sleep he was that tired, or the heavens he's soared through screaming! Oh, the things he told us about! And Alegra made them almost real so we could all be there again, just like she used to do when she was a psychiatrist! The stories, the places, the things . . ."

"Sounds like it was really something."

"It was nothing!" he came back vehemently. "It was all in the tears that wash your eyes, in the humming in your ears, in the taste of your own saliva. It was just a hallucination, Vyme! It wasn't real." Here his voice started cracking between the two octaves that were after it. "But that thing I told you about . . . huge . . . alive and dead at the same time, like a star . . . way in another galaxy. Well, he's seen it. And last night, but it wasn't real of course, but . . . I almost heard it . . . sing!" His eyes were huge and green and bright. I felt envious of anyone who could pull this reaction from kids like Alegra and Ratlit.

"So, we decided—" his voice fixed itself on the proper side of middle C—"after he went back to sleep, and we lay awake talking a while longer, that we'd try and help him get back out there. Because it's . . . wonderful!"

"That's fascinating." When I finished my call, I stood up from the desk. I'd been sitting on the corner. "After work I'll buy you dinner and you can tell me all about the things he showed you."

"He's still there, at Alegra's," Ratlit said—helplessly, I realized after a moment. "I'm going back there right after work."

"Oh," I said. I didn't seem to be invited.

"It's just a shame," Ratlit said when we came out of the office, "that he's so stupid." He glanced at the mess staining the concrete that had been a golden and shook his head.

I'd gone back to the books when Sandy stepped in. "All finished. What say we knock off for a beer or something, huh, boss?"

"All right," I said, surprised. Sandy was usually as social as he was handsome. "Want to talk about something?"

"Yeah." He looked relieved.

"That business this morning got to your head, huh?"

"Yeah," he repeated.

"There is a reason," I said as I made ready to go. "It's got something to do with the psychological part of being a golden. Meanness and stupidity, like everyone says. But however it makes them act here, it protects them from complete insanity at the twenty thousand light-year limit."

"Yeah. I know, I know." Sandy had started stepping uncomfortably from one boot to the other. "But that's not what I wanted to talk about."

"It isn't?"

"Um-um."

"Well?" I asked after a moment.

"It's that kid, the one you're gonna give the ship to."

"Ratlit?"

"Yeah."

"I haven't made up my mind about giving him the ship," I lied. "Besides, legally it's yours."

"You'll give it to him," Sandy said. "And I don't care. I mean not about the ship. But, boss, I gotta talk to you about that kid-boy."

Something about Sandy . . .

I'd never realized he'd thought of Ratlit as more than a general nuisance. Also, he seemed sincerely worried about me. I was curious. It took him all the way to the bar and through two beers—while I drank hot milk with honey—before he tongued and chewed what he wanted to say into shape.

"Boss, understand, I'm nearer Ratlit than you. Not only my age. My life's been more like his than yours has. You look at him like a son. To me, he's a younger brother: I taught him all the tricks. I don't understand him completely but I see him clearer than you do. He's had a hard time, but not as hard as you think. He's gonna take you—and I don't mean money—for everything he can."

Where the hell that came from I didn't know and didn't like. "He won't take anything I don't want to give."

"Boss?" Sandy suddenly asked. "You got kids of your own?"

"Nine," I said. "Did have. I don't see the ones who're left now, for which their parents have always been just as happy—except one. And she was sensible enough to go along with the rest, while she was alive."

"Oh." Sandy got quiet again. Suddenly he went scrambling in his overall pouch and pulled out a three-inch portapix. Those great, greasy hands that I was teaching to pick up an eggshell through a five-hundred-to-one-ratio waldo were clumsily fumbling at the push-pull levers. "I got kids," he said. "See. Seven of them."

And on the porta-pix screen was a milling, giggling group of little apes that couldn't have been anybody else's. All the younger ones lacked was acne. They even shuffled back and forth from one foot to the other. They began to wave, and the speaker in the back chirped: "Hi, Da! Hello, Da! Da, Mommy says to say we love you! Da, Da, come home soon!"

"I'm not with them now," he said throatily. "But I'm going back soon as I get enough money so I can take them all out of that hell-hole they're in now and get the whole family with a decent-sized proke-group. They're only twenty-three adults there now, and things were beginning to rub. That's why I left in the first place. It was getting so nobody could talk to anyone else. That's pretty rough on all our kids, thirty-two when I left. But soon I'll be able to fix that."

"On the salary I'm paying you?" This was the first I'd heard of any of this; that was my first reaction. My second, which I didn't voice, was: Then why the hell don't you take that ship and sell it somehow! Over forty and self-employed, the most romantic become momentarily practical.

Sandy's fist came down hard on the bar. "That's what I'm trying to say to you, boss! About you, about Ratlit. You've all got it in your heads that this, out here, is it! The end! Sure, you gotta accept limitations, but the right ones. Sure, you have to admit there are certain directions in which you can not go. But once you do that, you find there are others where you can go as far as you want. Look, I'm not gonna hang around the Star-pit all my life! And if I make my way back toward galactic center, make enough money so I can go home, raise my family the way I want, that's going forward, forward even from here. Not back."

"All right," I said. Quiet Sandy surprised me. I still wondered why he wasn't breaking his tail to get salvage on that ship that had just fallen into his hands, if getting back home with money in his pocket was that important. "I'm glad you told me about yourself. Now how does it all tie up with Ratlit?"

"Yeah. Ratlit." He put the porta-pix back in his overall pouch. "Boss, Ratlit is the kid your own could be. You want to give him the advice, friendship, and concern he's never had, that you couldn't give yours. But Ratlit is also the kid I was about ten years ago, started no place, with no destination, and no values to help figure out the way, mixed up in all the wrong things, mainly because he's not sure where the right ones are."

"I don't think you're that much like Ratlit," I told him. "I think you may wish you were. You've done a lot of the things Ratlit's done? Ever write a novel?"

"I tried to write a trilogy," Sandy said. "It was lousy. But it pushed some things off my chest. So I got something out of it, even if nobody else did, which is what's important. Because now I'm a better mechanic for it, boss. Until I admit to myself what I can't do, it's pretty hard to work on what I can. Same goes for Ratlit. You too. That's growing up. And one thing you can't do is help Ratlit by giving him a ship he can't fly."

Growing up brought back the picture. "Sandy, did you ever build an ecologarium when you were a kid?"

"No." The word had the puzzled inflection that means, "Don't-even-know-what-one-is.

"I didn't either," I told him. Then I grinned and punched him on the shoulder. "Maybe you're a little like me, too? Let's get back to work."

"Another thing," Sandy said, not looking very happy as he got off the stool. "Boss, that kid's gonna hurt you. I don't know how, but it's gonna seem like he hunted for how to make it hurt most, too. *That's* what I wanted to tell you, boss."

I was going to urge him to take the ship, but he handed me the keys back in the hangar before I could say anything, and walked away. When people who should be clearing up their own problems start giving you advice . . . well, there was something about Sandy I didn't like.

If I can't take long walks at night with company, I take them by myself. I was strolling by the Edge, the world-wind was low, and the Stellarplex, the huge heat-gathering mirror that's hung nine thousand miles off the Pit, was out. It looks vaguely like the moon used to look from Earth, only twice as big, perfectly silver, and during the three and a half days it faces us it's always full.

Then, up ahead where the fence was broken, I saw Ratlit kicking gravel over the Edge. He was leaning against a lamppost, his shirt ballooning and collapsing at his back.

"Hey, kid-boy! Isn't the golden still at Alegra's?"

Ratlit saw me and shrugged.

"What's the matter?" I asked when I reached him. "Ate dinner yet?"

He shrugged again. His body had the sort of ravenous metabolism that shows twenty-four hours without food. "Come on. I promised you a meal. Why so glum?"

"Make it something to drink."

"I know about your phony I.D.," I told him. "But we're going to eat. You can have milk, just like me."

No protests, no dissertation on the injustice of liquor laws. He started walking with me.

"Come on, kid-boy, talk to gramps. Don't you want your ship any more?"

Suddenly he clutched my forearm with white, bony fingers. My forearm is pretty thick, and he couldn't get his hands around it. "Vyme, you've got to make Sandy give it to me now! You've got to!"

"Kid-boy, talk to me."

"Alegra." He let go. "And the golden. Hate golden, Vyme. Always hate them. Because if you start to like one, and then start hating again, it's worse."

"What's going on? What are they doing?"

"He's talking. She's hallucinating. And neither one pays any attention to me."

"I see."

"You don't see. You don't understand about Alegra and me."

Then I was the only one who'd met the both of them who didn't. "I know you're very fond of each other." More could be said.

Ratlit said more. "We don't even like each other that much, Vyme. But we need each other. Since she's been here, I get her medicine for her. She's too sick to go out much now. And when I have bad changes, or sometimes bright recognitions, it doesn't matter, I bring them to her, and she builds pictures of them for me, and we explore them together and . . . learn about things. When she was a psychiatrist for the government, she learned an awful lot about how people tick. And she's got an awful lot to teach me, things I've got to know." Fifteen-year-old ex-psychiatrist drug addicts? Same sort of precocity that produces thirteen-year-old novelists. Get used to it. "I need her now almost as much as she needs her . . . medicine."

"Have you told the golden you've got him a ship?"

"You didn't say I could have it yet."

"Well, I say so right now. Why don't we go back there and tell him he can be on his way? If

we put it a little more politely, don't you think
that'll do the trick?"

He didn't say anything. His face just got back a
lot of its life.

"We'll go right after we eat. What the hell, I'll
buy you a drink. I may even have one with you."

Alegra's was blinding when we arrived. "Ratlit,
oh, you're back! Hello, Vyme! I'm so glad you're
both here! Everything is beautiful tonight!"

"The golden," Ratlit said. "Where's the golden?"

"He's not here." A momentary throb of sadness
dispelled with tortuous joy. "But he's coming
back!"

"Oh," Ratlit said. His voice echoed through the
long corridors of golden absence winding the
room. " 'Cause I got a ship for him. All his. Just
had a tune-up. He can leave any time he wants
to."

"Here's the keys," I said, taking them from my
pouch for dramatic effect. "Happen to have them
right here."

As I handed them to Ratlit there were fire-
works, applause, a fanfare of brasses. "Oh, that's
wonderful. Wonderful! Because guess what, Ratlit?
Guess what, Vyme?"

"I don't know," Ratlit said. "What?"

"I'm a golden too!" Alegra cried from the
shoulders of the cheering crowd that pushed its
way through more admiring thousands.

"Huh?"

"I, me, myself actually an honest-to-goodness
golden. I just found out today."

"You can't be," Ratlit said. "You're too old for
it just to show up now."

"Something about my medicine," Alegra explained. "It's dreadfully complicated." The walls
were papered with anatomical charts, music by

Stockhausen. "Something in my medicine kept it from coming out until now, until a golden could come to me, drawing it up and out of the depths of me, till it burst out, beautiful and wonderful and ... golden! Right now he's gone off to Carlson Labs with a urine sample for a final hormone check. They'll let him know in an hour, and he'll bring back my golden belt. But he's sure already. And when he comes back with it, I'm going to go with him to the galaxies, as his apprentice. We're going to find a cure for his sickness and something that will make it so I won't need my medicine any more. He says if you have all the universe to roam around in, you can find anything you look for. But you need it *all*—not just a cramped little cluster of a few billion stars off in a corner by itself. Oh, I'm free Ratlit, like you always wanted to be! While you were gone, he ... well, did something to me that was ... *golden*! It triggered my hormonal imbalance." The image came in through all five senses. Breaking the melodious ecstasy came the clatter of keys as Ratlit hurled them at the wall.

I left feeling pretty odd. Ratlit had started to go too, but Alegra called him back. "Oh, now don't go on like that, Ratty! Act your age. Won't you stay and do me one little last favor?"

So he stayed. When I untangled myself from the place and was walking home, I kept on remembering what Alegra had said about love.

Work next day went surprisingly smoothly. Poloscki called me up about ten and asked if I knew where Ratlit was because he hadn't been at work that day. "You're sure the kid isn't sick?"

I said I'd seen him last night and that he was probably all right. Poloscki made a disgusted sound and hung up.

Sandy left a few minutes early, as he'd been doing all week, to run over to the post office before it closed. He was expecting a letter from his group, he said. I felt strange about having given the ship away out from under him. It was sort of an immature thing to do. But he hadn't said anything about wanting it, and Ratlit was still doing Alegra favors, so maybe it would all work out for the best.

I thought about visiting Alegra that evening. But there was the last six months' paper work, still not finished. I went into the office, plugged in the computer and got ready to work late.

I was still at it sometime after eleven when the entrance light blinked, which meant somebody had opened the hangar door. I'd locked it. Sandy had the keys so he could come in early. So it was Sandy. I was ready for a break and all set to jaw with him awhile. He was always coming back to do a little work at odd hours. I waited for him to come into the office. But he didn't.

Then the needle on the power gauge, which had been hovering near zero with only the drain of the little office computer, swung up to seven. One of the big pieces of equipment had been cut in.

There was some cleanup work to do, but nothing for a piece that size. Frowning, I switched off the computer and stepped out of the office. The first great opening in the hangar roof was mostly blocked with the bulk of Ratlit's/Sandy's/my ship. Stellarplex light curved smoothly over one side, then snarled in the fine webbing of lifts, catwalks, haul-lines, and grappler rigging. The other two openings were empty, and thirty-meter circles of silver dropped through assembly riggings to the concrete floor. Then I saw Sandy.

He stood just inside the light from the last

opening, staring up at the Stellarplex, its glare lost in his ruined face. As he raised his left hand—when it started to move I thought it looked too big—light caught on the silver joints of the master-gauntlet he was wearing. I knew where the power was going.

As his hand went above his head, a shadow fell over him as a fifteen-foot slave talon swung from the darkness, its movement aping the master-glove. He dropped his hand in front of his face, fingers curved. Metal claws lowered about him, beginning to quiver. Something about . . . he was trying to kill himself!

I started running toward those hesitant, gaping claws, leaped into the grip, and reached over his shoulder to slap my forearm into the control glove, just as he squeezed. Like I said, my forearm is big, but when those claws came together, it was a tight fit. Sandy was crying.

"You stupid," I shouted, "inconsiderate, bird-brained, infantile—" at last I got the glove off "—puerile . . ." Then I said, "What the hell is the matter with you?"

Sandy was sitting on the floor now, his head hung between his shoulders. He stank.

"Look," I said, maneuvering the talon back into place with the gross-motion controls on the gauntlet's wrist, "if you want to go jump off the Edge, that's fine with me. Half the gate's down anyway. But don't come here and mess up my tools. You can squeeze your own head up a little, but you're not going to bust up my glove here. You're fired. Now tell me what's wrong."

"I knew it wasn't going to work. Wasn't even worth trying. I knew . . ." His voice was getting all mixed up with the sobs. "But I thought maybe . . ." Beside his left hand was the porta-pix, its screen cracked. And a crumpled piece of paper.

I turned off the glove, and the talons stopped humming twenty feet overhead. I picked up the paper and smoothed it out. I didn't mean to read it all the way through.

Dear Sanford,

Things have been difficult since you left but not too hard and I guess a lot of pressure is off everybody since you went away and the kids are getting used to your not being here though Bobbi-D cried a lot at first. She doesn't now. We got your letter and were glad to hear things had begun to settle down for you though Hank said you should have written before this and was very mad though Mary tried to calm him down but he just said, "When he married you all he married me too, damn it, and I've got just as much right to be angry at him as you have," which is true, Sanford, but I tell you what he said because it's a quote and I think you should know exactly what's being said, especially since it expresses something we all feel on one level or another. You said you might be able to send us a little money, if we wanted you home, which I think would be very good, the money I mean, though Laura said if I put that in the letter she would divorce us, but she won't, and like Hank I've got a right to say what I feel which is, Yes I think you should send money, especially after that unpleasant business just before you left. But we are all agreed we do not want you to come back. And would rather not have the money if that's what it meant.

That is hard but true. As you can gather your letter caused quite an upset here. I would like—which makes me different from the others but is why they wanted me to write this letter—to hear from you again and keep track of what you are doing because I used to love you very much and I never could hate you. But like Bobbi-D, I have stopped crying.

Sincerely—

The letter was signed "Joseph." In the lower corner were the names of the rest of the men and women of the group.

"Sandy?"

"I knew they wouldn't take me back. I didn't even really try, did I? But—"

"Sandy, get up."

"But the *children*," he whispered. "What's gonna happen to the children?"

And there was a sound from the other end of the hangar. Three stories up the side of the ship in the open hatchway, silvered by Stellarplex light, stood the golden, the one Ratlit and I had found on the street.

You remember what he looked like.

He and Alegra must have sneaked in while Sandy and I were struggling with the waldo. Probably they wanted to get away as soon as possible before Ratlit made real trouble, or before I changed my mind and got the keys back. All this ship-giving had been done without witnesses. The sound was the lift rising toward the hatchway. "The children . . ." Sandy whispered again.

The door opened, and a figure stepped out in the white light. Only it was Ratlit! It was Ratlit's red hair, his gold earring, his bouncy run as he started for the hatch. And there were links of yellow metal around his wrist.

Baffled, I heard the golden call: "Everything checks out inside, brother. She'll fly us anywhere."

And Ratlit cried, "I got the grapples all released, brother. Let's go!" Their voices echoed down through the hangar. Sandy raised his head, squinting.

As Ratlit leapt into the hatch, the golden caught his arm around the boy's shoulder. They stood a moment, gazing at one another, then Ratlit turned to look down into the hangar, back on the world he was about to leave. I couldn't tell if he knew we were there or not. Even as the hatch swung closed, the ship began to whistle.

I hauled Sandy back into the shock chamber. I hadn't even locked the door when the thunder came and my ears nearly split. I think the noise surprised Sandy out of himself. It broke something up in my head, but the pieces were falling wrong.

"Sandy," I said, "we've got to get going!"

"Huh?" He was fighting the drunkenness and probably his stomach too.

"I don't wanna go nowhere."

"You're going anyway. I'm sure as hell not going to leave you alone."

When we were halfway up the stairs I figured she wasn't there. I felt just the same. Was she with them in the ship?

"My medicine. Please can't you get my medicine? I've got to have my medicine, please, please ... please." I could just hear the small, high voice when I reached the door. I pushed it open.

Alegra lay on the mattress, pink eyes wide, white hair frizzled around her balding skull. She was incredibly scrawny, her uncut nails black as Sandy's nubs without the excuse of hours in a graphite-lubricated gauntlet. The translucency of her pigmentless skin under how-many-days of dirt made my flesh crawl. Her face drew in around her lips like the flesh about a scar. "My medicine, Vyme, is that you? You'll get my medicine for me, Vyme? Won't you get my medicine?" Her mouth wasn't moving, but the voice came on. She was too weak to project on any but the aural level. It was the first time I'd seen Alegra without her cloak of hallucination, and it brought me up short.

"Alegra," I said when I got hold of myself. "Ratlit and the golden went off on the ship!"

"Ratlit. Oh, nasty Ratty, awful little boy! He wouldn't get my medicine. But you'll get it for me, won't you, Vyme? I'm going to die in about ten minutes, Vyme. I don't want to die. Not like this. The world is so ugly and painful now. I don't want to die here."

"Don't you have any?" I stared around the room I hadn't seen since Drunk-roach lived there. It was a lot worse. Dried garbage, piled first in one corner, now covered half the floor. The rest was littered with papers, broken glass, and a spilled can of something unrecognizable for the mold.

"No. None here. Ratlit gets it from a man who hangs out in Gerg's over on Calle-X. Oh, Ratlit used to get it for me every day, such a nice little boy, every day he would bring me my lovely medicine, and I never had to leave my room at all. You go get it for me, Vyme!"

"It's the middle of the night, Alegra! Gerg's is closed, and Calle-X is all the way across the Pit anyway. Couldn't even get there in ten minutes, much less find this character and come back!"

"If I were well, Vyme, I'd fly you there in a cloud of light pulled by peacocks and porpoises, and you'd come back to hautboys and tambourines, bringing my beautiful medicine to me, in less than an eye's blink. But I'm sick now. And I'm going to die."

There was a twitch in the crinkled lid of one pink eye.

"Alegra, what happened!"

"Ratlit's insane!" she projected with shocking viciousness. I heard Sandy behind me catch his breath. "Insane at twenty thousand light-years, dead at twenty-five."

"But his golden belt ..."

"It was mine! It was my belt and he stole it. And he wouldn't get my medicine. Ratlit's not a golden. *I'm* a golden, Vyme! I can go anywhere, anywhere at all! I'm a golden golden golden ... But I'm sick now. I'm so sick."

"But didn't the golden know the belt was yours?"

"Him? Oh, he's so incredibly stupid! He would believe anything. The golden went to check some papers and get provisions and was gone all day, to get my belt. But you were here that night. I asked Ratlit to go get my medicine and take another sample to Carlson's for me. But neither of them came back till I was very sick, very weak. Ratlit found the golden, you see, told him that I'd changed my mind about going, and that he, Ratlit, was a golden as well, that he'd just been to Carlson's. So the golden gave him my belt and off they went."

"But how in the world would he believe a kid with a story like that?"

"You know how stupid a golden can be, Vyme.

As stupid as they can be mean. Besides, it doesn't matter to him if Ratlit dies. He doesn't care if Ratlit was telling the truth or not. The golden will live. When Ratlit starts drooling, throwing up blood, goes deaf first and blind last and dies, the golden won't even be sad. He's too stupid to feel sad. That's the way golden are. But I'm sad, Vyme, because no one will bring me my medicine."

My frustration had to lash at something; she was there. "You mean you didn't know what you were doing to Ratlit by leaving, Alegra? You mean you didn't know how much he wanted to get out, and how much he needed you at the same time? You couldn't see what it would do to him if you deprived him of the thing he needed and rubbed his nose in the thing he hated both at once? You couldn't guess that he'd pull something crazy? Oh, kid-girl, you talk about golden. You're the stupid one!"

"Not stupid," she projected quietly. "*Mean*, Vyme. I knew he'd try to do something. I just didn't think he'd succeed. Ratlit is really such a child."

The frustration, spent, became rolling sadness. "Couldn't you have waited just a little longer, Alegra? Couldn't you have worked out the leaving some other way, not hurt him so much?"

"I wanted to get out, Vyme, to keep going and not be trapped, to be free. Like Ratlit wanted, like you want, like Sandy wants, like golden. Only I was cruel. I had the chance to do it and I took it. Why is that bad, Vyme? Unless, of course, that's what being free means."

A twitch in the eyelid again. It closed. The other stayed open.

"Alegra—"

"I'm a golden, Vyme. A golden. And that's how golden are. But don't be mad at me, Vyme. Don't. Ratlit was mean too, not to give me my medi—"

The other eye closed. I closed mine too and tried to cry, but my tongue was pushing too hard on the roof of my mouth.

Sandy came to work the next day, and I didn't mention his being fired. The teletapes got hold of it, and the headlines tried to make the thing as sordid as possible:

X-CON TEEN-AGER (they didn't mention his novel)
SLAYS JUNKY SWEETHEART! DIES HORRIBLY!

They didn't mention the golden either. They never do.

Reporters pried around the hangar awhile, trying to get us to say the ship was stolen. Sandy came through pretty well. "It was his ship," he grunted, putting lubricant in the gauntlets. "I gave it to him."

"What are you gonna give a kid like that a ship for? Maybe you loaned it to him. 'Dies horrible death in borrowed ship.' That sounds okay."

"Gave it to him. Ask the boss." He turned back toward the scaffolding. "He witnessed."

"Look, even if you liked the kid, you're not saving him anything by covering up."

"I didn't like him," Sandy said. "But I gave him the ship."

"Thanks," I told Sandy when they left, not sure what I was thanking him for but still feeling very grateful. "I'll do you a favor back."

A week later Sandy came in and said, "Boss, I want my favor."

I narrowed my eyes against his belligerent tone. "So you're gonna quit at last. Can you finish out the week?"

He looked embarrassed, and his hands started moving around in his overall pouch. "Well, yeah.

I am gonna leave. But not right away, boss. It is getting a little hard for me to take, out here."

"You'll get used to it," I said. "You know there's something about you that's, well, a lot like me. I learned. You will too."

Sandy shook his head. "I don't think I want to." His hand came out of his pocket. "See, I got a ticket." In his dirty fingers was a metal-banded card. "In four weeks I'm going back in from the Star-pit. Only I didn't want to tell you just now, because, well, I did want this favor, boss."

I was really surprised. "You're not going back to your group," I said. "What are you going to do?"

He shrugged. "Get a job, I don't know. There're other groups. Maybe I've grown up a little bit." His fists went way down into his pouch, and he started to shift his weight back and forth on his feet. "About that favor, boss."

"What is it?"

"I got to talking to this kid outside. He's really had it rough, Vyme." That was the first and last time Sandy ever called me by name, though I'd asked him to enough times before. "And he could use a job."

A laugh got all set to come out of me. But it didn't, because the look on his ugly face, behind the belligerence, was so vulnerable and intense. Vulnerable? But Sandy had his ticket; Sandy was going on.

"Send him to Poloscki's," I said. "Probably needs an extra grease monkey. Now let me get back to work, huh?"

"Could you take him over there?" Sandy said very quickly. "That's the favor, boss."

"Sandy, I'm awfully busy." I looked at him again. "Oh, all right."

"Hey, boss," Sandy said as I slid from behind

the desk, "remember that thing you asked me if I ever had when I was a kid?"

It took a moment to come back to me. "You mean an ecologarium?"

"Yeah. That's the word." He grinned. "The kid-boy's got one. He's right outside, waiting for you."

"He's got it with him?"

Sandy nodded.

I walked toward the hangar door picturing some kid lugging around a six-by-six plastic cage.

Outside the boy was sitting on a fuel hydrant. I'd put a few trees there, and the "day"-light from the illumination tubes arcing the street dappled the gravel around him.

He was about fourteen, with copper skin and curly black hair. I saw why Sandy wanted me to go with him about the job. Around his waist, as he sat hunched over on the hydrant with his toes spread on the metal base-flange, was a wide-linked, yellow belt: golden.

He was looking through an odd jewel-and-brass thing that hung from a chain around his neck.

"Hey."

He looked up. There were spots of light on his blue-black hair.

"You need a job?"

He blinked.

"My name's-Vyme. What's yours?"

"You call me An." The voice was even, detached, with an inflection that is golden.

I frowned. "Nickname?"

He nodded.

"And really?"

"Androcles."

"Oh." My oldest kid is dead. I know it because I have all sorts of official papers saying so. But sometimes it's hard to remember. And it doesn't matter whether the hair is black, white, or red. "Well, let's see if we can put you to work somewhere. Come on." An stood up, eyes fixed on me, suspicion hiding behind high glitter. "What's the thing around your neck?"

His eyes struck it and bounced back to my face. "Cousin?" he asked.

"Huh?" Then I remembered the golden slang. "Oh, sure. First cousins. Brothers if you want."

"Brother," An said. Then a smile came tumbling out of his face, silent and volcanic. He began loping beside me as we started off toward Poloscki's. "This—" he held up the thing on the chain "—is an ecologarium. Want to see?" His diction was clipped, precise, and detached. But when an expression caught on his face, it was unsettlingly intense.

"Oh, a little one. With microorganisms?"

An nodded.

"Sure. Let's have a look."

The hair on the back of his neck pawed the chain as he bent to remove it.

I held it up to see.

Some blue liquid, a fairly large air bubble, and a glob of black-speckled jell in a transparent globe, the size of an eyeball; it was set in two rings, one within the other, pivoted so the globe turned in all directions. Mounted on the outside ring was a curved tongue of metal at the top of which was a small tube with a pin-sized lens. The tube was threaded into a bushing, and I guess you used it to look at what was going on in the sphere.

"Self-contained," explained An. "The only thing needed to keep the whole thing going is light. Just about any frequency will do, except way up on the blue end. And the shell cuts that out."

I looked through the brass eyepiece.

I'd swear there were over a hundred life forms with five to fifty stages each: spores, zygotes, seeds, eggs, growing and developing through larvae, pupae, buds, reproducing through sex, syzygy, fission. And the whole ecological cycle took about two minutes.

Spongy masses like red lotuses clung to the air bubble. Every few seconds one would expel a cloud of black things like wrinkled bits of carbon paper into the gas where they were attacked by tiny motes I could hardly see even with the lens. Black became silver. It fell back to the liquid like globules of mercury, and coursed toward the jelly that was emitting a froth of bubbles. Something in the froth made the silver beads reverse direction. They reddened, sent out threads and alveoli, until they reached the main bubble again as lotuses.

The reason the lotuses didn't crowd each other out was because every eight or nine seconds a swarm of green paramecia devoured most of them. I couldn't tell where they came from; I never saw one of them split or get eaten, but they must have had something to do with the thornballs—if only because there were either thornballs or paramecia floating in the liquid, but never both at once.

A black spore in the jelly wiggled, then burst the surface as a white worm. Exhausted, it laid a couple of eggs, rested until it developed fins and a tail, then swam to the bubbles where it laid more eggs among the lotuses. Its fins grew larger, its tail shriveled, splotches of orange and blue appeared, till it took off like a weird butterfly to sail around the inside of the bubble. The motes that silvered the black offspring of the lotus must have eaten the parti-colored fan because it just grew thinner and frailer till it disappeared. The eggs by the lotus would hatch into bloated fish forms that swam back through the froth to vomit a glob of jelly on the mass at the bottom, then collapse. The first eggs didn't do much except turn into black spores when they were covered with enough jelly.

All this was going on amidst a kaleidoscope of frail, wilting flowers and blooming jeweled webs, vines and worms, warts and jellyfish, symbiotes and saprophytes, while rainbow herds of algae careened back and forth like glittering confetti. One rough-rinded galoot, so big you could see him without the eyepiece, squatted on the wall, feeding on jelly, batting his eye-spots while the tide surged through quivering tears of gills.

I blinked as I took it from my eye.

"That looks complicated." I handed it back to him.

"Not really." He slipped it around his neck. "Took me two weeks with a notebook to get the whole thing figured out. You saw the big fellow?"

"The one who winked?"

"Yes. Its reproductive cycle is about two hours, which trips you up at first. Everything else goes so fast. But once you see him mate with the thing that looks like a spider web with sequins—same creature, different sex—and watch the offspring aggregate into paramecia, then dissolve again, the whole thing falls into—"

"One creature!" I said. "The whole thing is a single creature!"

An nodded vigorously. "Has to be to stay self-contained." The grin on his face whipped away like a snapped window-shade. A very serious look was underneath. "Even after I saw the big fellow mate, it took me a week to understand it was all one."

"But if goofus and the fishnet have paramecia—" I began. It seemed logical when I made the guess.

"You've seen one before."

I shook my head. "Not like that one, anyway. I once saw something similar, but it was much bigger, about six feet across."

An's seriousness was replaced by horror. I mean he really started to shake. "How could you . . . *ever* even *see* all the . . . stuff inside, much less *catalogue* it? You say . . . *this* is complicated?"

"Hey, relax. Relax!" I said. He did. Like that. "It was much simpler," I explained and went on to describe the one our kids had made so many years ago as best I remembered.

"Oh," An said at last, his face set in its original impassivity. "It wasn't microorganisms. Simple. Yes." He looked at the pavement. "Very simple." When he looked up, another expression had scrambled his features. It took a moment to identify. "I don't see the point at all."

There was surprising physical surety in the boy's movement; his nervousness was a cat's, not a human's. But it was one of the psychological qualities of golden.

"Well," I said, "it showed the kids a picture of the way the cycles of life progress."

An rattled his chain. "That is why they gave us these things. But everything in the one you had was so primitive. It wasn't a very good picture."

"Don't knock it," I told him. "When I was a kid, all I had was an ant colony. I got my infantile *Weltanschauung* watching a bunch of bugs running around between two plates of glass. I think I would have been better prepared by a couple of hungry rats on a treadmill. Or maybe a torus-shaped fish tank alternating sharks with schools of piranhas: Get them all chasing around after each other real fast—"

"Ecology wouldn't balance," An said. "You'd need snails to get rid of the waste. Then a lot of plants to reoxygenate the water, and some sort of herbivore to keep down the plants because they'd tend to choke out everything since neither the sharks nor the piranhas would eat them." Kids and their damn literal minds. "If the herbivores had some way to keep the sharks off, then you might do it."

"What's wrong with the first one I described?"

The explanation worked around the muscles of his face. "The lizards, the segment worms, the plants, worts, all their cycles were completely circular. They were born, grew up, reproduced, maybe took care of the kids awhile, then died. Their only function was reproduction. That's a pretty awful picture." He made an unintelligible face.

There was something about this wise-alecky kid who was golden, younger than Alegra, older than Ratlit, I liked.

"There are stages in here," An tapped his globe with his pinky nail, "that don't get started on their most important functions till after they've reproduced and grown up through a couple more metamorphoses as well. Those little green worms are a sterile end stage of the blue feathery things. But they put out free phosphates that the algae live on. Everything else, just about, lives on the algae—except the thorn-balls. They eat the worms when they die. There're phagocytes in there that injest the dust-things when they get out of the bubble and start infecting the liquid." All at once he got very excited. "Each of us in the class got one of these! They made us figure them out! Then we had to prepare these recordings on whether the reproductive process was the primary function in life or an adjunctive one." Something white frothed the corners of his mouth. "I think grown-ups should just *leave* their kids the hell

alone, go on and do something *else*, stop bothering us! That's what I said! That's what I *told*
them!" He stopped, his tongue flicked the foam at
the cusp of his lips; he seemed all right again.

"Sometimes," I said evenly, "if you leave them
alone and forget about them, you end up with
monsters who aren't kids any more. If you'd been
left alone, you wouldn't have had a chance to put
your two cents in in the first place and you
wouldn't have that thing around your neck." And
he was really trying to follow what I was saying.
A moment past his rage, his face was as open and
receptive as a two-year-old's. God, I want to stop
thinking about Antoni!

"That's not what I mean." He wrapped his
arms around his shoulders and bit on his forearm
pensively.

"An—you're not stupid, kid-boy. You're cocky,
but I don't think you're mean. You're golden."
There was all my resentment, out now, Ratlit.
There it is, Alegra. I didn't grow up with the
word, so it meant something different to me. An
looked up to ingest any meaning. The toothmarks
were white on his skin, then red around that.
"How long have you been one?"

He watched me, arms still folded. "They found
out when I was seven."

"That long ago?"

"Yes." He turned and started walking again. "I
was very precocious."

"Oh." I nodded. "Just about half your life then.
How's it been, little brother, being a golden?"

An dropped his arms. "They take you away
from your group a lot of times." He shrugged.
"Special classes. Training programs. I'm psychotic."

"I never would have guessed." What would you
call Ratlit? What would you call Alegra?

"I know it shows. But it gets us through the

psychic pressures at the reality breakdown at twenty thousand light-years. It really does. For the past few years, though, they've been planting the psychosis artificially, pretty far down in the preconscious, so it doesn't affect our ordinary behavior as much as it does the older ones. They can use this process on anybody whose hormone system is even close to golden. They can get a lot more and a lot better quality golden that way than just waiting for us to pop up by accident."

As I laughed, something else struck me. "Just what do you need a job out here for, though? Why not hitch out with some cousin or get a job on one of the intergalactics as an apprentice?"

"I have a job in another galaxy. There'll be a ship stopping for me in two months to take me out. A whole lot of Star-pits have been established in galaxies halfway to Un-dok. I'll be going back and forth, managing roboi-equipment, doing managerial work. I thought it would be a good idea to get some practical experience out here before I left."

"Precocious," I nodded. "Look, even with roboi-equipment you have to know one hell of a lot about the inside of how many different kinds of keeler drives. You're not going to get that kind of experience in two months as a grease monkey. And roboi-equipment? I don't even have any in my place. Poloscki's got some, but I don't think you'll get your hands on it."

"I know a good deal already," An said with strained modesty.

"Yeah?" I asked him a not too difficult question and got an adequate answer. Made me feel better that he didn't come back with something really brilliant. I did know more than he did. "Where'd you learn?"

"They gave me the information the same way they implanted my psychosis."

"You're pretty good for your age." Dear old Luna Vocational! Well, maybe educational methods have improved. "Come to think of it, I was just as old as you when I started playing around with those keeler models. Dozens and dozens of helical inserts—"

"And those oily organum sensitives in all that graphite? Yes, brother! But I've never even had my hands in a waldo."

I frowned. "Hell, when I was younger than you, I could—" I stopped. "Of course, with roboi-equipment, you don't need them. But it's not a bad thing to know how they work, just in case."

"That's why I want a job." He hooked one finger on his chain. "Brother-in-law Sandy and I got to talking, so I asked him about working here. He said you might help me get in someplace."

"I'm glad he did. My place only handles big ships, and it's all waldo. Me and an assistant can do the whole thing. Poloscki's place is smaller, but handles both inter- and intra-galactic jobs, so you get more variety and a bigger crew. You find Poloscki, say I sent you, tell what you can do and why you're out here. Belt or no, you'll probably get something better than a monkey."

"Thanks, brother."

We turned off Calle-D. Poloscki's hangar was ahead. Dull thunder sounded over the roof as a ship departed.

"As soon as I despair of the younger generation," I told him, "one of you kids comes by and I start to think there's hope. Granted you're a psychopath, you're a lot better than some of your older, distant relations."

An looked up at me, apprehensive.

"You've never had a run-in with some of your

cousins out here. But don't be surprised if you're dead tomorrow and your job's been inherited by some character who decided to split your head open to check on what's inside. I try to get used to you, behaving like something that isn't even savage. But, boy-kid, can your kind really mess up a guy's picture of the universe."

"And what the hell do you expect us to act like?" An shot back. Spittle glittered on his lips again. "What would *you* do if you were trapped like *us*?"

"Huh?" I said questioningly. "*You*, trapped?"

"Look." A spasm passed over his shoulders. "The psycho-technician who made sure I was properly psychotic *wasn't* a golden, *brother*! You *pay* us to bring back the weapons, dad! *We* don't fight your damn wars, *grampa*! *You're* the ones who take us away from our groups, say we're *too* valuable to submit to *your* laws, then deny us our heredity because we don't *breed* true, no-relative-of *mine*!"

"Now, wait a minute!"

An snatched the chain from around his neck and held it taut in front of him. His voice ground to a whisper, his eyes glittered. "I strangled one of my classmates with this chain, the one I've got in my hands now." One by one, his features blanked all expression. "They took it away from me for a week, as punishment for killing that little girl."

The whisper stopped decibels above silence, then went on evenly. "Out here, nobody will punish me. And my reflexes are faster than yours."

Fear lashed my anger as I followed the insanity flickering in his eyes.

"Now!" He made a quick motion with his hands; I ducked. "I give it to you!" He flung the chain toward me. Reflexively I caught it. An turned away instantly and stalked into Poloscki's.

When I burst through the rattling hangar door at my place, the lift was coming down. Sandy yelled through the mesh walls, "Did he get the job?"

"Probably," I yelled back, going toward the office.

I heard the cage settle on the silicon cushion. Sandy was at my side a moment later, grinning. "So how do you like my brother-in-law, Androcles?"

"Brother-in-law?" I remembered An using the phrase, but I'd thought it was part of the slang golden. Something about the way Sandy said it though. "He's your *real* brother-in-law?"

"He's Joey's kid brother. I didn't want to say anything until after you met him." Sandy came along with me toward the office door. "Joey wrote me again and said since An was coming out here he'd tell him to stop by and see me and maybe I could help him out."

"Now how the hell am I supposed to know who Joey is?" I pushed open the door. It banged the wall.

"He's one of my husbands, the one who wrote me that letter you told me you'd read."

"Oh, yeah. Him." I started stacking papers.

"I thought it was pretty nice of him after all that to tell An to look me up when he got out here. It means that there's still somebody left who doesn't think I'm a complete waste. So what do you think of Androcles?"

"He's quite a boy." I scooped up the mail that had come in after lunch, started to go through it but put it down to hunt for my coveralls.

"An used to come visit us when he got his one weekend a month off from his training program as golden," Sandy was going on. "Joey's and An's parents lived in the reeds near the estuary. But we lived back up the canyon by Chroma Falls. An and Joey were pretty close, even though Joey's my age and An was only eight or nine back then. I guess Joey was the only one who really knew what An was going through, since they were both golden."

Surprised and shocked, I turned back to the desk. "You were married to a golden?" One of the letters on the top of the pile was addressed to Alegra from Carlson's Labs. I had a carton of the kids' junk in the locker and had gotten the mail—there wasn't much—sent to the hangar, as though I were waiting for somebody to come for it.

"Yeah," Sandy said, surprised at my surprise. "Joey."

So I wouldn't stand there gaping, I picked up Alegra's letter.

"Since the traits that are golden are polychromazoic, it dies out if they only breed with each other. There's a big campaign back in galactic center to encourage them to join heterogeneous proke-groups."

"Like bluepoint Siamese cats, huh?" I ran my blackened thumbnail through the seal.

"That's right. But there're *not* animals, boss. I remember what they put that kid-boy through for psychotic reinforcement of the factors that were golden to make sure they stuck. It tore me up to hear him talk about it when he'd visit us."

I pulled a porta-pix out of Alegra's envelope. Carlson's tries to personalize its messages.

"I'm sure glad they can erase the conscious memory from the kids' minds when they have to do that sort of stuff."

"Small blessings and all that." I flipped the porta-pix on.

Personalized but mass produced: "... blessed addit ..." the little speaker echoed me. Poloscki and I had used Carlson's a couple of times, I know. I guess every other mechanic up here had too. The porta-pix had started in the middle. Now it hummed back to the beginning.

"You know," Sandy went on, "Joey was different, yeah, sort of dense about some things ..."

"Alegra," beamed the chic, grandmotherly type Carlson's always uses for messages of this sort, "we were so glad to receive the urine sample you sent us by Mr. Ratlit last Thursday ..."

"... even so, Joey was one of the sweetest men or women I've ever known. He was the easiest person in the group to live with. Maybe it was because he was away a lot ..."

"... and now, just a week later—remember, Carlson's gives results immediately and confirms them by personalized porta-pix in seven days—we are happy to tell you that there will be a blessed addition to your group. However ..."

"... All right, he was different, reacted funny to a lot of things. But nothing like this rank, destructive stupidity you find out here at the Star-pit ..."

"... the paternity is not Mr. Ratlit's. If you are interested, for your eugenic records, in further information, please send us other possible urine samples from the men in your group, and we will be glad to confirm paternity ..."

"... I can't understand the way people act out here, boss. And that's why I'm pushing on."

"... Thank you so much for letting us give you this wonderful news. Remember, when in doubt, call Carlson's."

I said to Sandy, "You were married with—you loved a golden?"

Unbidden, the porta-pix began again. I flipped it off without looking.

"Sandy," I said, "you were hired because you were a fair mechanic and you kept off my back. Do what you're paid for. Get out of here."

"Oh. Sure, boss." He backed quickly from the office.

I sat down.

Maybe I'm old fashioned, but when someone runs off and abandons a sick girl like that, it gets me. That was the trip to Carlson's, the one last little favor Ratlit never came back from. On-the-spot results, and formal confirmation in seven days. In her physical condition, pregnancy would have been as fatal as the withdrawal. And she was too ill for any abortive method I know of not to kill her. On-the-spot results. Ratlit must have known all that too when he got the results back, the results that Alegra was probably afraid of, the results she sent him to find. Ratlit knew Alegra was going to die anyway. And so he stole a golden belt. "Loving someone, I mean really loving someone—" Alegra had said. When someone runs off and leaves a sick girl like that, there's got to be a reason. It came together for me like two fissionables. The explosion cut some moorings in my head I thought were pretty solidly fixed.

I pulled out the books, plugged in the computer, unplugged it, put the books away, and stared into the ecologarium in my fist.

Among the swimming, flying, crawling things, mating, giving birth, growing, changing, busy at whatever their business was, I picked out those dead-end, green worms. I hadn't noticed them before because they were at the very edge of things, bumping against the wall. After they released their free phosphates and got tired of butting at the shell, they turned on each other and tore themselves to pieces.

Fear and anger is a bad combination in me.

I came close to being killed by a golden once, through that meanness and stupidity.

The same meanness and stupidity that killed Alegra and Ratlit.

And now when this damn kid threatens to—I mean at first I had thought he was threatening to—

I reached Gerg's a few minutes after the daylights went out and the street lamps came on. But I'd stopped in nearly a dozen places on the way. I remember trying to explain to a sailor from a star-shuttle who was just stopping over at the Star-pit for the first time and was all upset because one woman golden had just attacked another with a broken glass; I remember saying to the three-headed bulge of his shoulder, ". . . an ant colony! You know what it is, two pieces of glass with dirt between them, and you can see all the little ants make tunnels and hatch eggs and stuff. When I was a kid, I had an ant colony . . ." I started to shake my hand in his face. The chain from the ecologarium was tangled up in my fingers.

"Look." He caught my wrist and put it down on the counter. "It's all right now, pal. Just relax."

"You look," I said as he turned away. "When I was a kid, all I had was an *ant* colony!"

He turned back and leaned his rusty elbow on the bar. "Okay," he said affably. Then he made the most stupid and frustrating mistake he possibly could have just then. "What about your aunt?"

"My mother—"

"I thought you were telling me about your aunt?"

"Naw," I said. "My aunt, she drank too much. This is about my mother."

"All right. Your mother then."

"My mother, see, she always worried about me, getting sick and things. I got sick a lot when I was a little kid. She made me mad! Used to go down and watch the ships take off from the place they called the Brooklyn Navy Yards. They were ships that went to the stars."

The sailor's Oriental face grinned. "Yeah, me too. Used to watch 'em when I was a kid."

"But it was raining, and she wouldn't let me go."

"Aw, that's too bad. Little rain never hurt a kid. Why didn't she call up and have it turned off so you could go out? Too busy to pay attention to you, huh? One of my old men was like that."

"Both of mine were," I said. "But not my ma. She was all over me all the time when she was there. But she made me mad!"

He nodded with real concern. "Wouldn't turn off the rain."

"Naw, couldn't. You didn't grow up where I did, narrow-minded, dark-side world. No modern conveniences."

"Off the main trading routes, huh?"

"Way off. She wouldn't let me go out, and that made me mad."

He was still nodding.

"So I broke it!" My fist came down hard on the counter, and the plastic globe in its brass cage clacked on the wood. "Broke it! Sand, glass all over the rug, on the windowsill!"

"What'd you break?"

"Smashed it, stamped on it, threw sand whenever she tried to make me stop!"

"Sand? You lived on a beach? We had a beach when I was a kid. A beach is nice for kids. What'd you break?"

"Let all the damn bugs out. Bugs in everything for days. Let 'em all out."

"Didn't have no bugs on our beach. But you said you were off the main trading routes."

"Let 'em *out*!" I banged my fist again. "Let *every*body out, whether they like it or not! It's their problem whether they make it, not mine! Don't care, I don't—" I was laughing now.

"She let you go out, and you didn't care?"

My hand came down on top of the metal cage, hard. I caught my breath at the pain. "On our beach," I said, turning my palm up to look. There were red marks across it. "There weren't any bugs on our beach." Then I started shaking.

"You mean you were just putting me on, before, about the bugs. Hey, are you all right?"

". . . broke it," I whispered. Then I smashed fist and globe and chain into the side of the counter. "Let 'em *out*!" I whirled away, clutching my bruised hand against my stomach.

"*Watch* it, kid-boy!"

"I'm not a kid-boy!" I shouted. "You think I'm some stupid, half-crazy kid!"

"So you're older than me. Okay?"

"I'm not a kid any more!"

"So you're ten years older than Sirius, all right? Quiet down, or they'll kick us out."

I bulled out of Gerg's. A couple of people came after me because I didn't watch where I was going. I don't know who won, but I remember somebody yelling, "Get out! Get out!" It may have been me.

I remember later, staggering under the mercury street lamp, the world-wind slapping my face, stars swarming back and forth below me, gravel sliding under my boots, the toes inches over the Edge. The gravel clicked down the metal siding, the sound terribly clear as I reeled in the loud wind, shaking my arm against the night.

As I brought my hand back, the wind lashed the cold chain across my cheek and the bridge of my nose. I lurched back, trying to claw it away. But it stayed all tangled on my fingers while the globe swung, gleaming in the street light. The wind roared. Gravel chattered down the siding.

Later, I remember the hangar door ajar, stumbling into the darkness, so that in a moment I was held from plummeting into nothing only by my own footsteps, as black swerved around me. I stopped when my hip hit a workbench. I pawed around under the lip of the table till I found a switch. In the dim orange light, racked along the back of the bench in their plastic shock-cases, were the row of master-gauntlets. I slipped one out and slid my hand into it.

"Who's over there?"

"Go 'way, Sandy." I turned from the bench, switched up the power on the wrist controls. Somewhere in the dark above, a fifteen-foot slave-hand hummed to life.

"Sorry, buster. This isn't Sandy. Put that down and get away from there."

I squinted as the figure approached in the orange light, hand extended. I saw the vibra-gun and didn't bother to look at the face.

Then the gun went down. "Vyme, baby? That you? What the hell are you doing here this hour of the night?"

"Poloscki?"

"Who'd you think it was?"

"Is this your—?" I looked around, shook my head. "But I thought it was my—" I shook my head again.

Poloscki sniffed. "Hey, have you been a naughty kid-boy tonight!"

I swung my hand, and the slave-hand overhead careened twenty feet.

The gun jumped. "Look, you mess up my waldo and I will kill you, don't care who you are! Take that thing off."

"Very funny." I brought the talon down where I could see it clawing shadow.

"Come on, Vyme. I'm serious. Turn it off and put it down. You're a mess now and you don't know what you're doing."

"That kid, the golden. Did you give him a job?"

"Sure. He said you sent him. Smart little so-and-so. He rehulled a little yacht with the roboi-anamechaniakatasthysizer, just to show me what he could do. If I knew a few more people who could handle them that well I'd go all roboi. He's not worth a damn with a waldo, but as long as he's got that little green light in front of him, he's fine."

I brought the talons down another ten feet so that the spider hung between us. "Well, I happen to be very handy with a waldo, Poloscki."

"Vyme, you're gonna get *hurrrt* . . ."

"Poloscki," I said, "will you stop coming on like an overprotective aunt? I don't need another one."

"You're very drunk, Vyme."

"Yeah. But I'm no clumsy kid-boy who is going to mess up your equipment."

"If you do, you'll be—"

"Shut up and watch." I pulled the chain out of my pouch and tossed it onto the concrete floor. In the orange light you couldn't tell whether the cage was brass or silver.

"What's that?"

The claws came down, and the fine-point tips, millimeters above the floor, closed on the ecologarium.

"Oh hey! I haven't seen one of those since I was ten. What are you going to do with it? Those are five-hundred-to-one strength, you know. You're gonna break it."

"That's right. Break this one too."

"Aw, come on. Let me see it first."

I lifted the globe. "Could be an eggshell," I said. "Drunk or sober I can handle this damn equipment, Poloscki."

"I haven't seen one for years. Used to have one."

"You mean it wasn't spirited back from some distant galaxy by golden, from some technology beyond our limited ken?"

"Product of the home spiral. Been around since the fifties."

I raised it over Poloscki's extended hand.

"They're supposed to be very educational. What do you want to break it for?"

"I never saw one."

"You came from someplace off the routes, didn't you? They weren't that common. Don't break it."

"I want to."

"Why, Vyme?"

Something got wedged in my throat. "Because I want to get out, and if it's not that globe, it's gonna be somebody's head." Inside the gauntlet my hand began to quiver. The talons jerked. Poloscki caught the globe and jumped back.

"Vyme!"

"I'm hanging here at the Edge." My voice kept getting caught on the things in my throat. "I'm useless, with a bunch of monsters and fools!" The talons swung, contracted, clashed on each other. "And then when the children . . . when the *children* get so bad you can't even reach them . . ." The claw opened, reached for Poloscki who jumped back in the half-dark.

"Damn it, Vyme—"

". . . can't even reach the children any more." The talon stopped shaking, came slowly back, knotting. "I want to break something and get out. Very childishly, yes. Because nobody is paying any attention to *me*." The claw jumped. "Even when I'm trying to help. I *don't* want to hurt anybody any *more*. I *swear* it, so help me, I swear—"

"Vyme, take off the glove and listen!"

I raised the slave-hand because it was about to scrape the cement.

"Vyme, I want to pay some attention to you." Slowly Poloscki walked back into the orange light. "You've been sending me kids for five years now, coming around and checking up on them, helping them out of the stupid scrapes they get in. They haven't all been Ratlits. I like kids too. That's why I take them on. I think what you do is pretty great. Part of me loves kids. Another part of me loves you."

"Aw, Poloscki ..." I shook my head. Somewhere disgust began.

"It doesn't embarrass me. I love you a little and wouldn't mind loving you a lot. More than once I've thought about asking you to start a group."

"*Please*, Poloscki. I've had too many weird things happen to me this week. Not tonight, huh?" I then turned the power off in the glove.

"Love shouldn't frighten you, no matter when or how it comes, Vyme. Don't run from it. A marriage between us? Yeah, it would be a little hard for somebody like you, at first. But you'd get used to it before long. Then when kids came around, there'd be two—"

"I'll send Sandy over," I said. "He's the big-hearted marrying kind. Maybe he's about ready to try again." I pulled off the glove.

"Vyme, don't go out like that. Stay for just a minute!"

"Poloscki," I said, "I'm just not that God damn drunk!" I threw the glove on the table.

"Please, Vyme."

"You're gonna use your gun to keep me here?"

"Don't be like—"

"I hope the kids I send over here appreciate you more than I do right now. I'm sorry I busted in here. Good-night!"

I turned from the table.

Nine thousand miles away the Stellarplex turned too. Circles of silver dropped through the roof. Behind the metal cage of the relaxed slave claw I saw Polocki's large, injured eyes, circles of crushed turquoise, glistening now.

And nine feet away someone said, "Ma'am?"

Poloscki glanced over her shoulder. "An, you awake?"

An stepped into the silver light, rubbing his neck. "That office chair is pretty hard, sister."

"He's here?" I asked.

"Sure," Poloscki said. "He didn't have any place to stay so I let him sleep in the office while I finished up some work in the back. Vyme, I meant what I said. Leave if you want, but not like this. Untwist."

"Poloscki," I said, "you're very sweet, you're fun in bed, and a good mechanic too. But I've been there before. Asking me to join a group is like asking me to do something obscene. I know what I'm worth."

"I'm also a good businesswoman. Don't think that didn't enter my head when I thought about marrying you." An came and stood beside her. He was breathing hard, the way an animal does when you wake it all of a sudden.

"Poloscki, you said it, I didn't: I'm a mess. That's why I'm not with my own group now."

"You're not always like this. I've never seen you touch a drop before."

"For a while," I said, "it happened with disgusting frequency. Why do you think my group dropped me?"

"Must have been a while ago. I've known you a long time. So you've grown up since then. Now it only happens every half dozen years or so. Congratulations. Come have some coffee. An, run into the office and plug in the pot. I showed you where it was." An turned like something blown by the world-wind and was gone in shadow. "Come on," Poloscki said. She took my arm, and I came with her. Before we left the light, I saw my reflection in the polished steel tool-cabinet.

"Aw, no." I pulled away from her. "No, I better go home now."

"Why? An's making coffee."

"The kid. I don't want the kid to see me like this."

"He already has. Won't hurt him. Come on."

When I walked into Poloscki's office, I felt I didn't have a damn thing left. No. I had one. I decided to give it away.

When An turned to me with the cup, I put my hands on his shoulders. He jumped, but not enough to spill the coffee. "First and last bit of alcoholic advice for the evening, kid-boy. Even if you are crazy, don't go around telling people who are not golden how they've trapped you. That's like going to Earth and complimenting a nigger on how well he sings and dances and his great sense of rhythm. He may be able to tap seven with one hand against thirteen with the other while whistling a tone row. It still shows a remarkable naïvete about the way things are." That's one of the other things known throughout the galaxy about the world I come from. When I say primitive, I mean primitive.

An ducked from under my hands, put the coffee on the desk, and turned back. "I didn't say you trapped us."

"You said we treated you lousy and exploited you, which we may, and that this trapped you—"

"I said you exploited us, which you do, *and* that we were trapped. I *didn't* say by what."

Poloscki sat down on the desk, picked up my coffee and sipped it.

I raised my head. "All right. Tell me how you're trapped."

"Oh, I'm sorry," Poloscki said. "I started drinking your coffee."

"Shut up. How are you trapped, An?"

He moved his shoulders around as though he was trying to get them comfortable. "It started in Tyber-44 cluster. Golden were coming back with really bad psychic shock."

"Yes. I heard about it. That was a few years back."

An's face started to twitch; the muscles around his eyes twisted below the skin. "*Something* out there . . ."

I put my hand on the back of his neck, my thumb in the soft spot behind his ear and began to stroke, the way you get a cat to calm down. "Take it easy. Just tell me."

"Thanks," An said and bent his head forward. "We found them first in Tyber-44, but then they turned up all *over*, on half the planets in every galaxy that could support any life, and a lot more that shouldn't have been able to at all." His breathing grew coarser. I kept rubbing, and it slowed again. "I guess we have such a funny psychology that working with them, studying them, even thinking about them too much ... there was something about them that changes our sense of reality. The shock was bad."

"An," I said, "to be trapped, there has to be somewhere you can't go. For it to bug you, there has to be something else around that can."

He nodded under my hand, then straightened up. "I'm all right now. Just tired. You want to know where and what?"

Poloscki had put down the coffee now and was dangling the chain. An whirled to stare.

"Where?" he said. "Other universes."

"Galaxies farther out?" asked Poloscki.

"No. Completely different matrices of time and space." Staring at the swinging ball seemed to calm him even more. "No physical or temporal connection to this one at all."

"A sort of parallel—"

"Parallel? Hell!" It was almost a drawl. "There's nothing parallel about them. Out of the billions-to-the-billionth of them, most are hundreds of times the size of ours and empty. There are a few, though, whose entire spatial extent is even smaller than this galaxy. Some of them are completely dense to us, because even though there seems to be matter in them, distributed more or less as in this universe, there's no electromagnetic activity at all. No radio waves, no heat, no light." The globe swung; the voice was a whisper.

I closed my fist around the globe and took it from Poloscki. "How do you know about them? Who brings back the information? Who is it who can get out?"

Blinking. An looked back at me.

When he told me, I began to laugh. To accommodate the shifting reality tensions, the psychotic personality that is golden is totally labile. An laughed with me, not knowing why. He explained through his torrential hysteria how with the micro-micro surgical techniques from Tyber-44 they had read much of the information from a direct examination of the creature's nervous system, which covered its surface like velvet. It could take intense cold or heat, a range of pressure from vacuum to hundreds of pounds per square millimeter; but a fairly small amount of ultraviolet destroyed the neural synapses, and it died. They were small and deceptively organic because in an organic environment they appeared to breathe and eat. They had four sexes, two of which carried the young. They had clusters of retractable sense organs that first appeared to be eyes, but were sensitive to twelve distinct senses, stimulation for three of which didn't even exist in our continuum. They traveled around on four suction cups when using kinetic motion for ordinary traversal of space, were small, and looked furry. The only way to make them jump universes was to scare the life out of them. At which point they just disappeared.

An kneaded his stomach under his belt to ease the pain from so much laughter. "Working with them at Tyber-44 just cracked up a whole bunch of golden." He leaned against the desk, panting and grinning. "They had to be sent home for therapy. We still can't think about them directly, but it's easier for us to control what we think about than for you; that's part of being golden. I even had one of them for a pet, up until yesterday. The damn creatures are either totally apathetic, or vicious. Mine was a baby, all white and soft." He held out his arms. "Yesterday it bit me and disappeared." On his wrist there was a bluish place centered on which was a crescent of pinpricks. "Lucky it was a baby. The bits infect easily."

Poloscki started drinking from my cup again as An and I started laughing all over.

As I walked back that night, black coffee slopped in my belly.

There are certain directions in which you cannot go. Choose one in which you can move as far as you want. Sandy said that? He did. And there was something about Sandy, very much like someone golden. It doesn't matter how, he's going on.

Under a street lamp I stopped and lifted up the ecologarium. The reproductive function, was it primary or adjunctive? If, I thought with the whiskey lucidity always suspect at dawn, you consider the whole ecological balance a single organism, it's adjunctive, a vital reparative process along with sleeping and eating, to the primary process which is living, working, growing. I put the chain around my neck.

I was still half soused, and it felt bad. But I howled. Androcles, is drunken laughter appropriate to mourn all my dead children? Perhaps not. But tell me, Ratlit; tell me Alegra: what better way to launch my live ones who are golden into night? I don't know. I know I laughed. Then I put my fists into my overall pouch and crunched homeward along the Edge, while on my left the world-wind roared.